Hawaii Five-Go!

Collect all the books in the Luna Bay *series*

*coming soon

Luna Bay

a ♥ ROXY GiRL series

BOOK FIVE

Hawaii Five-Go!

by Francess Lantz

HarperEntertainment
An Imprint of HarperCollinsPublishers

This book is a work of fiction. References to real people, events, establishments, organizations, or locales are intended only to provide a sense of authenticity, and are used fictitiously. All other characters, and all incidents and dialogue, are drawn from the author's imagination and are not to be construed as real.

FIRST EDITION

Designed by Jackie McKee

ISBN 0-06-057374-0

WBC/OPM 10 9 8 7 6 5 4 3 2 1

For Jodie, Frank, and Liv

Acknowledgments

With thanks to: Hope Innelli, Kaipo Schwab,
Bruce Hale, Mark Rauzon, Lise Tseu, Sandy Salisbury,
Jeffery McGraw, and Kendra Marcus.

Cricket is bouncing in her seat like a hyperactive two-year-old. The elderly couple across the aisle frowns disapprovingly, but Cricket can't help herself. In fact, she can't figure out how anyone on the airplane can *not* be jumping up and down.

Don't they realize we've just landed in Hawaii? she wonders.

The island of Oahu, to be specific. Home of Sunset Beach, Waimea, Pipeline, Backdoor, and about a zillion other world-famous surf spots.

The flight attendants open the doors and Cricket leaps to her feet, accidentally slamming into her friend Luna in the process.

"Whoa, girl," Luna laughs. "Don't injure me before we even leave the plane. I have to save myself for those coral reefs."

Cricket giggles nervously. Oahu's powerful waves

break over sharp lava rocks and shallow coral reefs. One false move and a surfer could wind up with some seriously shredded skin. It's a scary thought, and Cricket wonders if she's ready to ride the heavy, take-no-prisoners waves of the island's North Shore. But she quickly pushes the thought out of her mind. She and her four best friends wouldn't be here if *Water Woman* magazine didn't think they were up to the challenge.

Cricket presses into the crowded aisle. In the row behind her, Isobel is doing the same. "Let me out of here," Isobel mutters impatiently. "I've gone without eating sweets for an entire month and I'm ready to be photographed. I didn't even eat my grandmother's famous Christmas cookies. Now that's sacrifice!"

Isobel's words remind Cricket that surfing isn't the only challenge in store for them. *Water Woman* has brought the girls to Hawaii over winter break to photograph them for the magazine's spring swimwear issue. The girls are going to surf—and pose—in bikinis manufactured by some of the hottest surfwear companies in the world.

Cricket knows she should feel honored, but all she really feels is nervous. *I'm no model,* she thinks for at least the hundredth time that day.

She gazes down at her body and assesses its glam potential. She's as skinny as a flagpole, flat-chested, and has a spattering of freckles across her nose that she'd gladly trade in for an even tan. But then she considers her smile—it's just like her mom's. And her arms—she has the perfectly-defined arms of a swimmer. Maybe she doesn't have Kanani's curves, Isobel's flawless toffee skin, Rae's gorgeous strawberry-blond hair, or Luna's slender legs, but a great smile and shapely arms ought to do it, she tells herself.

Isobel is busy eyeing herself as well. She loves her body most when she's surfing. She has the ideal build for the sport—muscular and toned in some places, soft in others, the right mix of strength and buoyancy. But this week, in anticipation of the photo shoot, she just can't seem to stop thinking about her weight. "Honestly, Cricket, I just look at an Oreo cookie and gain two pounds. Of course, you wouldn't know anything about *that*."

Cricket just shrugs. It's true she can eat anything she wants and never gain weight. But so what? "I have the perfect solution," she jokes. "Give me a few extra pounds for my chest and we'll both be happy!"

"Stick together, girls," calls Dierdre Hoag, *Water Woman*'s fashion editor. She's the person who'll be organizing the photo sessions and writing the article. "Look for the person holding the *Water Woman* sign and go directly to her."

"Do not pass go. Do not collect two hundred dollars," Cricket mutters under her breath.

Luna snickers. "She's like a kindergarten teacher or something. I mean, what does she think we're going to do? Run off with some local boy and never be seen again?"

"That wouldn't be so bad," Rae declares. "Some Hawaiian hottie with wavy black hair and dimples."

While the girls are joking around, the aisle begins to clear out. "Get a move on," Luna's mother urges.

Luna's mom, Cate Martin, is a former world champion surfer and the co-owner of Shoreline Surf Shop. She's also about the coolest mother Cricket has ever met. That's why Cricket doesn't mind that Cate has come along as the girls' chaperone.

The girls move eagerly toward the door. In the jetway they meet up with Josh Collard, the *Water Woman* staff photographer who'll be shooting the article. He's in his late twenties, Cricket figures, with unruly brown hair, rumpled clothing, and glasses.

"Ready to catch some waves?" Cricket asks him.

"Not me," he replies, clearing his throat as he pushes his glasses up his nose. "I can't swim."

"What?" Isobel gasps, overhearing. "But I've seen your photos in the magazine. How did you get those amazing water shots?"

He considers her question, then finally raises his eyebrows and says, "I paddle out on a boogie board and pray."

Cricket shoots Isobel a glance—is this guy weird or what?—and continues through the jetway. With each step her heart seems to rise and then—yes!—she's stepping into the terminal, officially in Hawaii at last.

"We're here! We're really here!" she cries. As usual, her words come out so fast, they almost blur together. Giggling, she reaches out to hug the first friend she sees.

It's Rae. She laughs and proclaims, "Watch out, Oahu! The Crescent Cove girls are on the scene!"

It *is* kind of mind-blowing, Cricket realizes. It's only been a year and a half since she started surfing with Luna, Rae, Isobel, and Kanani. In that time they've become best friends, surfed on the high school team, competed in some important contests, and—in the case of Luna, Rae, and Isobel—found sponsors. Now, thanks to the buzz that's been developing around the girls, *Water Woman* has brought them all to the North Shore.

What's next? Cricket wonders. She can't wait to find out!

"Girls! Over here!" It's Dierdre, clapping her hands and clucking like a mother hen as she ushers the girls toward a young woman with blond dreadlocks. The woman is holding a *Water Woman* magazine sign and her arms are draped with leis, necklaces made of flowers, in this case the fragrant pikake flower.

"Aloha!" she says with a smile. "I'm Suzie Goldberg. I write and edit articles on the North Shore contest scene for *Water Woman*. Welcome to Hawaii!" She places a lei over each girl's head, and another on Cate.

Cricket grins, hopping from foot to foot as she breathes in the wonderful scent. When she's excited, she can't stand still, and right now she is definitely excited. Her eyes are drawn to the nearest window where she catches a glimpse of flowering bushes and swaying

5

palm trees. It's hard to believe it was cold and rainy when they left California that morning. She can't wait to soak in some sunshine!

"What are we waiting for?" she asks impatiently.

Suzie laughs. "I like your enthusiasm! Let's collect your bags and boards and hit the highway."

"The highway?" Cricket repeats. "I was figuring we'd be bouncing down dirt roads through the jungle and stuff."

"Yeah," Rae agrees. "I mean, this is Hawaii, right? Not L.A."

Suzie just smiles indulgently. "Girls," she says, "you've got a lot to learn about Oahu."

Thirty minutes later, Cricket and her friends are sitting in a traffic jam in downtown Honolulu.

"This is just wrong!" Cricket wails. "Here we are in Hawaii with our surfboards strapped to the roof of a killer red Xterra. We're supposed to be at the beach, not stuck in rush-hour traffic!"

"Like I said, you have a lot to learn about Oahu," Suzie chuckles from the driver's seat. "Honolulu is a major metropolis. But things will change once we reach the Kamehameha Highway."

Luna's mother drives next to them in the other rental car, a yellow Xterra. Dierdre is in the passenger seat, and Luna and Josh are riding in back.

Kanani rolls down the window. "Aloha!" she shouts, waggling her fist with her thumb and pinkie extended—the traditional Hawaiian hang-loose sign.

"Aloha, wahines!" Luna calls. "Don't you just love this sweet Hawaiian air?" She feigns a coughing fit.

"Ka-me-ha-me-ha come-up-ha soon-ha!" Cricket exclaims in a silly voice. "Then we get plenty fresh air, big surf, Hawaiian hotties!"

Suddenly Suzie hits the master window control, sending all the windows scooting upward.

"Hey!" Cricket cries, pulling her head in. "Why'd you do that?"

"Let me give you a piece of advice," Suzie says seriously. "If you want to make friends with those Hawaiian hotties—or any locals for that matter—don't go making fun of their language. And don't make fun of King Kamehameha, either."

"Who's he?" Isobel asks.

"Kamehameha was the first king to rule all the Hawaiian islands in the late eighteenth century," Kanani pipes up.

"Very good," Suzie says. "Someone's been doing her homework."

"Kanani's half-Hawaiian," Rae explains.

"Oh, really?" Suzie asks with interest. "Were you born here?"

Kanani is explaining about her Hawaiian birthfather and the white birthmother who put her up for adoption in California when she was only a month old, but Cricket isn't really listening. She feels embarrassed at being reprimanded and a little annoyed.

Who does Suzie think she is? she wonders irritably. *With those blond dreads and white skin, she certainly isn't Hawaiian.*

Cricket reaches into her carry-on bag and pulls out a king-size bag of M&M's. Her friends call her a junk food junkie, and she can't deny it. She loves anything sweet. She pops a few M&M's in her mouth and crunches happily. *When life gets you down,* she tells herself, *just add chocolate.*

She passes the M&M's around and stares out the window at the endless skyscrapers, apartment buildings, and resort hotels. Finally, after what feels like forever, the traffic starts to thin out. They drive by Pearl Harbor and finally Suzie turns onto the Kamehameha Highway. Soon they're cruising through fields of pineapple and sugarcane. Palm trees line the road and, in the distance, massive green mountains reach for the sky.

By the time they take the turnoff for the North Shore town of Haleiwa, Cricket is tapping her foot wildly. She can't stand sitting still, especially when she knows they're getting close to surf. But as they cruise down Haleiwa's main street, she stops tapping and starts staring. The street is lined with surf shops, clothing stores, and funky restaurants. Even more interesting, there are young, tanned surfers everywhere, many of them strolling along in bathing suits, flip-flops, and nothing else.

"Did you see that dude?" Rae asks, gazing dreamily at a muscular boy with shoulder-length blond hair who is coming out of a surf shop.

"How about *him*?" Cricket counters, drooling over a wiry Asian guy with spiky black hair and an earring.

"Hey, isn't that Taj Burrow?" Isobel gasps, unabashedly pointing at the famous surfer.

"Stop pointing!" Kanani cries. "You look like a tourist!"

"I *am* a tourist," Isobel declares with a shrug.

"Hardly," Rae protests. "In case you forgot, we're soon-to-be-famous fashion models."

"Oh, my God! It's Flea!" Kanani cries, totally losing her cool. "He's only one of the best big-wave surfers in the world!"

Flea is strolling along the street with a gorgeous girl, munching on something that looks like a cup of rainbow-colored ice. "What's he eating?" Cricket asks.

"Shave ice," Suzie says. "A Hawaiian favorite. Let's stop and get some."

Soon they're all standing at the counter of Sunset Sensations, ordering cups of shave ice drenched in syrup with flavors like mango, coconut, passion fruit, and bubble gum. Cricket slurps happily as they drive out of Haleiwa.

Now the highway is a coastal two-lane road, crawling with surfboard-stacked cars and jeeps. The sun is setting as Suzie pulls off onto a bumpy dirt road.

"Now this is more like it!" Cricket exclaims.

A beautiful white house surrounded by red-flowering hibiscus bushes comes into view. "Girls, this is going to be your home for the next week," Suzie says, pulling to a stop.

The girls gasp and leap out of the car. Once inside, they scope out the bedrooms. Josh gets his own room, and Dierdre shares a room with Luna's mom. There are two bedrooms left—one with two beds and one with three.

"Share a room with me, Cricket," Kanani says, nudging her friend.

"Okay," Cricket replies. She dumps her bag on the nearest bed.

"Come check out the lanai," Suzie calls.

The girls follow Suzie onto a porch that overlooks a palm-tree-lined white sand beach. In the distance, the ocean appears dark blue under the fading light. A breeze is blowing and the faraway sound of crashing waves mixes with the calls of the tropical birds.

"Girls, I want all of you to get unpacked," Dierdre says in her best mother-hen voice. "Then we'll go into town for some dinner."

The girls obey like good little chicks—all except Cricket, who remains on the lanai, gazing pensively at the ocean. She has more important things on her mind than organizing her clothing. She's thinking about her dad.

Last month, on Cricket's sixteenth birthday, her estranged father, legendary Malibu surfer Chet Connolly, sent her a bar of homemade surf wax. There was no return address, but the package was postmarked Haleiwa, Hawaii.

"I know you're out there somewhere, Dad," she whispers. "And I'm going to find you."

"Cricket?"

She spins around to find Kanani walking toward her.

"All unpacked like a good little surfer girl?" Cricket asks.

But Kanani isn't smiling. "I have a secret to tell you," she says softly. "Before we left, my mom gave me the name of my birthfather. She didn't have his address or any other information about him. But she had his name. Liko Kaunolu."

Cricket gives her friend a meaningful hug. She knows how much Kanani wants to find her birthfather—just as much as Cricket wants to find her own long-lost dad.

"I haven't told the others," Kanani continues. "I just don't want to turn this into a big deal, you know? I mean, I might not be able to find him. But . . . well, I knew you'd understand."

Cricket nods. "If I can help you in any way, just ask, okay?"

"Likewise."

"Girls!" Dierdre shouts, suddenly appearing at the door to the lanai. "What are you doing out here? We're leaving for town in exactly five minutes."

The girls exchange a look. "Coming, Mother," Cricket mutters and, laughing, they head inside to join the others.

2

*L*ater that night, Cricket is lying in bed, biting her nails as she stares at the ceiling. In the next bed, Kanani snores softly. Cricket sighs and glances at the bedside clock. Almost midnight. Dierdre sent the girls to bed at exactly ten o'clock, promising she'd wake them before dawn so they could go surfing. But Cricket can't sleep. She's just too excited. Tomorrow she'll get her first taste of Hawaiian surf. And who knows? Maybe she'll even take the first step toward tracking down her father.

Twelve-oh-one. Cricket gets up and tiptoes out into the hall. Silence. Slowly and quietly, she opens the door to the lanai and steps outside. A warm breeze is blowing and the air smells like flowers. Drawn by the enticing sound of crashing waves, Cricket walks down the stairs to the sand.

She stops under a palm tree and stares, entranced,

at the half-moon hanging over the water. Is her father on the North Shore somewhere, looking at this same ocean, this same moon?

Suddenly, Cricket hears a soft crunching sound behind her. Out of the darkness a lilting voice says, "I'd move away from those trees if I were you. There's rats living up in the palm fronds."

Cricket shrieks and leaps back. The voice laughs with delight. Then a slender figure steps out of the shadows. "What you doin' out so late, haole girl?"

Heart pounding, Cricket tries to focus. It's a boy, a teenage boy! He's tall and wiry, and dressed only in baggy surfer trunks. His dark, wavy hair hangs below his shoulders and his white teeth gleam in the moonlight.

"I—I could ask you the same thing," Cricket says, her words tumbling over each other like falling dominoes. She always talks fast, but when she's scared or excited—and she's a little of both right now—she's a total motormouth. "I mean, what are you doing out here trying to scare people? There should be a law or something." She pauses for a microsecond. "Are there really rats in the trees?"

The boy laughs again. "Yes. So I'd suggest we move, yeah?"

They take a few steps toward the water. Now she can see the taut muscles on his arms and chest, and his long, handsome face.

"To answer your question," he continues, "I live up the beach about a half-mile. I like to walk by the water at night. It's quiet and peaceful—no tourists." He gives her a look. "Well, usually."

"What have you got against tourists?" she asks. "And what's a—what did you call me? A howl-ee?"

"*Haole* means 'white person.' As for my opinion of tourists, that's a long story." He flashes a smile. "Where are you from?"

"California. A town called Crescent Cove."

"And now you've come to Hawaii to work on your tan."

"No way!" she protests. "I'm here to surf."

"Oh, you're a surfer girl," he says with a chuckle. "Maybe you had a lesson or two in Waikiki, yeah?"

"You really think you've got me figured out, don't you?" she snaps. "Well, for your information, I've been surfing since I was thirteen and I'm good. Really good. As a matter of fact, I'm going to be a pro someday."

"That right? Well, excuse me, haole girl. I misjudged you. So what's your favorite break on the North Shore?"

"Well," she admits, "I haven't actually surfed here yet. I mean, I just got in today. But I'm going to be surfing lots of places. Not only that, *Water Woman* magazine is photographing my friends and me for their spring swimwear preview."

"You're a model?" he says, eyeing her skeptically.

Cricket's shoulders droop. She knows she's not a *model* model. It's so obvious, it's laughable. "Yeah, well," she mutters, "they picked me for my surfing talent, not my runway sneer."

Or did they pick her because of her friends? It never occurred to her before, but now it seems as if they might have. She's pretty and all, especially on a good hair day, but not as pretty as the other girls, and she's definitely not as successful either. She doesn't have a sponsor and her biggest accomplishment so far has been placing fourth at the ASA Western Championship. If it wasn't for the whole sisterhood thing going on between her, Luna, Rae, Isobel, and Kanani, she probably wouldn't be in Hawaii at all.

"Hey, what's wrong?" the boy asks, turning his head to look into her face. "I didn't say you weren't pretty."

She shrugs.

"Look at those eyes. There's fire burning in them. And forget about sneering. When you smile just right, your lips form a perfect heart. Did you know that, surfer girl?"

Cricket smiles self-consciously.

"My name is Kainoa. What's yours?"

"Cricket."

He laughs. "It suits you." Then he looks at her and says, "Maybe this is my lucky night, Cricket. I found myself a California girl to take my blues away." He moves closer as he sings softly, " 'California dreaming . . . ' "

Cricket puts her hand in the middle of his chest and gives him a shove.

"Hey!" he yells, staggering back. "What was that for?"

"You think just because I'm a tourist I'm going to

fall for that stupid pickup line? Well, forget it. You may be a local boy, but you're not so special."

Kainoa's face darkens. A stab of fear slices through Cricket. She doesn't know this guy from Adam. Here they are alone on the beach, not a soul in sight. Who knows what could happen?

But suddenly, he bursts out laughing. "What did I tell you? There's a fire burning in you," he says and reaches out to her with his index finger. "Get too close and—" He makes a sizzling sound and pulls his hand away.

Cricket feels herself relax. But then she hears a rustling sound from under the palm trees. She turns just in time to see something dark and hairy—and much bigger than a rat—scurrying toward her. In fact, she realizes with a start, it has a rat in its mouth!

"Eeee!" she wails, levitating into the air.

The furry, weasellike creature freezes, turns, and scrambles back into the shadows.

Kainoa doubles over with laughter. "That's the first time I ever saw a mongoose run from a cricket!"

"A *what*?"

He stands up, still snickering. "So long, haole girl. Maybe I will see you out in the water, yeah?"

With that, he strolls away, leaving Cricket with her mouth hanging open and her heart dancing inside her chest.

* * *

"Does everyone have on sunscreen?" Deirdre asks as Cate and the girls gather on the lanai the next morning. Josh is there, too, his camera bag slung over his shoulder.

"Why aren't we wearing the new bikinis?" Cricket asks.

"This isn't an official photo session," Deirdre explains. "We're just checking out the location and giving you girls a chance to get used to the break. Then tomorrow we'll go back and photograph you surfing in the new suits."

"Where are we going?" Luna asks.

"Lili'u's Reef," Deirdre replies. "It's just a short hike up the beach."

Rae looks disappointed. "I've never heard of it. Why don't we go to Velzyland or Log Cabins or—"

"The title of this feature is going to be 'Secret Spots,'" Deirdre explains. "It's a pun, you see. We're going to photograph you surfing at some local spots—the kind of places the tourists don't know about. Plus, you'll be wearing bathing suits that hold up to real-life surfing conditions. No matter how hard you shred, they won't fall off and expose your secret spots. Get it?"

The girls laugh and Cate says, "Pretty clever."

"My editor thought so, too," Deirdre says with a satisfied smile. "Now grab your boards and let's go surfing."

Cricket steps cautiously as they walk between the

palm trees, keeping an eye out for rats and mongooses. Then she thinks about Kainoa and her pulse quickens. That long hair, that smile, those muscles! He was hot!

Would he look as handsome in the daylight? she wonders.

And then she reminds herself she doesn't care. She's not interested in a boy that cocky and condescending.

Cricket runs to catch up with her friends. The sun is rising and the ocean is a beautiful sparkling blue. They walk on another five minutes, laughing and talking excitedly. Then, up ahead, they spot the break—a fast, hollow right that builds up about fifty yards offshore.

Cricket stops and stares. The waves are only four or five feet high, but they're breaking with a speed and ferocity she's never seen before. As she watches, a surfer takes off and shoots across the wave face like a bottle rocket.

"Whoa!" Cricket breathes.

"You said it," Luna agrees.

"There's a channel to the right," Cate says, pointing to the spot where a surfer is paddling out. "Everyone follow me and stick together."

Cricket's stomach tightens as she straps on her leash. Is she ready for this? All she knows for sure is she's not going to wimp out—not in front of her friends, and definitely not in front of Deirdre and Josh.

Okay, then, she tells herself, popping a square of bubble gum into her mouth and chomping nervously. *Ready or not, here I come.*

Cricket splashes into the warm water and starts paddling behind Cate and Luna. Rae, Kanani, and Isobel bring up the rear. Cricket grins. It feels fantastic to be paddling without a wet suit! She glides effortlessly through the channel, feeling like a prisoner who has just been released from her chains.

When they reach the break, Cate and the girls join the lineup. There are four guys bobbing on their boards—all dark-skinned young men with black hair. Locals, Cricket presumes. She meets the eye of the beefy surfer closest to her and smiles. He stares back, unblinking.

Cricket shoots a quizzical look at Isobel, who shrugs uncertainly. Cricket glances over her shoulder. A set is rolling in. She feels a prickle of fear slide down her neck, but when she's nervous, she can't sit still. So she chomps her gum and starts paddling.

"Go, Cricket!" she hears Luna call.

She feels the wave rise quickly beneath her, hops to her feet, she cranks a hard bottom turn. But as she straightens out, another surfer drops in on her. It's the beefy guy who stared at her earlier.

"Hey!" she shouts, assuming he'll pull out when he realizes she's there. Instead, he cuts back toward the curl, forcing her up the face of the wave. He slices right just as Cricket is sucked over the falls. With a scream, she tumbles through the air and lands with such force that she labors to catch her breath.

The whitewater rolls her around and suddenly she whacks against something hard. The coral! She struggles to the surface and grabs her board just as another wave is breaking. She duck-dives under it, then paddles fast back into the channel.

Cate is waiting for her. "Are you okay?" she asks.

Cricket's left thigh is burning. She looks down and sees where the coral scraped her just below her bathing suit. "That jerk dropped in on me," she says angrily.

"The locals demand respect," Cate says. "That's just the way it is in the islands. But these guys are a little over-the-top. They don't want us here, and they aren't subtle about letting us know it."

"So what do we do now?" Cricket asks.

"Let's give it another try. But play it cool, okay? Give the local guys the big waves and we'll take the leftovers—at least until we can prove to them we're serious surfers."

Chomping nervously on her gum, Cricket paddles back into the lineup. She sees Rae take off on a wave, only to be cut off by one of the locals. Cricket hesitates, wondering if she dares to surf another wave. Then she notices a local guy with a ponytail and a goatee paddling into the lineup. As he glides past her he growls under his breath, "Go back to Waikiki, haole."

Cricket feels a rush of anger. What's with these guys anyway? Back home, some of the local surfers can be pretty territorial, but they're like teddy bears compared to these Hawaiian boys.

Just then Cricket sees a familiar figure paddling out through the channel. Can it be? Yes, it's Kainoa! Cricket's heart rises. She lifts her arm over her head and waves eagerly.

"Kainoa!" she calls. "Over here!"

"You know him?" Kanani asks with surprise.

"I couldn't sleep last night so I walked down to the beach. I met a local boy there. *That* local boy."

"Sweet. Maybe he can help us make friends with the other guys out here."

But instead of paddling over to Cricket, Kainoa makes a point of going around her—far around her. In fact, he doesn't even glance her way.

"Are you sure that's the guy?" Kanani asks.

Cricket takes a good look at Kainoa, who is now sitting on his board, bantering with his friends. Yes, she decides, he *is* just as handsome in the daylight. "Definitely," she says.

"Go over and talk to him," Kanani suggests.

Cricket shrugs. After the way Kainoa ignored her, she's not sure what to think. Then she notices a new set rolling in. Fearful of getting hassled, she lets wave after wave go under her, watching jealously as the locals rip on one perfect grinder after another.

Then, when the set is almost over, she sees one last wave heading her way. Back home, she'd probably think it was too small to even bother with, but remembering what Cate told her, she starts paddling. She drops in and bottom-turns. Even though the wave is small, it's got some juice. Eagerly, she heads up to the lip—only to see a boy taking off in front of her.

It's Kainoa! To her horror, he stands up right in front of her. She tries to cut back, but it's too late. The nose of her surfboard smacks against the back of his board and she wipes out. But not Kainoa. As Cricket hits the water, he glances over his shoulder at her. Then, with his arms pumping the air, he lets out a triumphant whoop and disappears down the line.

"Plate lunch? What's that?" Cricket asks as the girls follow Deirdre into a restaurant called Puka's Plate Lunch in downtown Haleiwa.

"Lunch on a plate, of course," Luna replies.

Rae snickers. "Better than lunch on the floor."

"It's a local favorite," Luna's mom explains as they sit down. "Your choice of meat or fish, two scoops of rice, and a scoop of macaroni salad. After a morning of surfing, it really hits the spot."

"Is that what we were doing?" Cricket asks with disgust. "It felt more like wiping out to me."

"Well, what do you expect?" Isobel cries. "Those guys were snaking our waves."

"*Who* was snaking your waves?" Suzie Goldberg asks, joining them at the table.

"Some local boys," Deirdre explains.

"They were totally rude," Rae adds. "Dropping in on us, dissing us. What did we ever do to them?"

"We're supposed to photograph there tomorrow," Josh grumbles. "I sincerely hope they don't show up."

"Wait a minute," Suzie says. "Where were you?"

"A break called Lili'u's Reef," Deirdre replies. "It's just down the beach from where we're staying."

"Oh," Suzie says with a knowing nod.

Just then the waitress arrives and they all order plate lunch and sodas. After she leaves, Suzie explains, "Lili'u's Reef is named after Queen Lili'uokalani, Hawaii's last reigning monarch. It's sort of a secret spot. Not many tourists know about it, and the locals want to keep it that way."

"Well, that's too bad," Deirdre pipes up. "My editor told me to find beautiful, out-of-the way places to photograph the girls. He wants local color, and that's what I'm going to give him."

"How did you even find this spot?" Suzie asks. "I doubt it's in many guidebooks."

"When I got the assignment, I e-mailed every surfer in *Water Woman*'s address book and asked them for Oahu's best-kept secrets. Lili'u's Reef was mentioned by a couple of them."

Just then, the waitress appears with the food. Cricket isn't a fish lover, so she's ordered chicken on her plate lunch. It's covered with sweet teriyaki sauce and tastes great. Beside her, Kanani is digging into her mahi mahi. Luna and her mom are eating some sort of white fish.

"What's that?" Cricket asks.

"Ahi tuna," Luna says. "Want to taste it?"

Cricket hesitates, but Luna thrusts a forkful toward her. She takes a tentative bite. To her surprise, it's delicious!

For the next five minutes, the only sounds at the table are chewing and sipping. Then Suzie turns to Deirdre. "You're not planning on revealing the location of Lili'u's Reef in your article, are you?"

"Why not?" she responds. "Every magazine in the world has a spring swimsuit issue. My job is to make *Water Woman*'s spring preview stand out from the pack. And since this *is* a magazine about water sports, that's what we want to emphasize."

Suzie sighs. "The major spots—Sunset, Waimea, Pipeline—are already overcrowded with surfers from around the globe. You're not going to make any friends on the North Shore if you encourage tourists to flock to one of the few breaks the locals have managed to keep for themselves."

Deirdre snorts a laugh. "Oh, come on, Suzie! It's a little late to be saving Oahu from tourism. Besides, a ten-page fashion spread in *Water Woman* isn't going to make a serious difference to what goes on over here. But if we come up with something that's hip and edgy, it *will* make a difference to our sales figures. That's what it's all about for me."

Cricket taps her fork against her plate, thinking it over. Oahu is filled with tourists, and tourists spend money. So why wouldn't the locals want to do everything in their power to encourage more people to come to the island? Okay, so the roads are a little congested and the surf spots are pretty crowded. Isn't that a small price to pay for prosperity?

She knows that's what her mother would say. Mom works for the Crescent Cove Chamber of Commerce. She spends forty hours a week (no, Cricket reminds herself, make that sixty—she's a total workaholic) trying to convince people to come to Crescent Cove and spend money. If she could convince *Water Woman* to shoot a fashion spread there, she'd be jumping for joy. And she wouldn't mind revealing a few local surf spots to do it.

"Okay, I've got an idea," Suzie says. "If you want the locals to welcome you to their surf spots, you've got to show them you're not out to exploit them or their island. The best way to do that is to get to know them and let them get to know you. I suggest throwing a luau."

"A luau?" Deirdre repeats. "You mean one of those outdoor events they put on at the big hotels—with hula dancers and all that?"

"That's the tourist version of a luau. I'm talking about a little island beach party. We'll roast some chicken, play some music, talk story—"

"Talk story?" Cricket asks. "What's that?"

"It means 'shoot the breeze.' Chew the fat. Talk together," Suzie explains. She turns to Deirdre. "Do you think you could find a few bucks in your expense account for something like that?"

Deirdre nods. "I'll have to call my editor, but I think he'll go for it."

"What do we do in the meantime?" Josh asks, cleaning his glasses with his napkin. "Twiddle our thumbs?"

"How about surf?" Cricket suggests. "Not at Lili'u's Reef, but, you know, one of the famous spots. Like Kammieland or Gas Chambers or—"

"Not today. I want to get some shots of you girls standing in front of a quaint North Shore shop, eating shave ice, that sort of thing."

"Shave ice!" Rae exclaims. "I could go for some of that!"

"Good," Deirdre replies, "because the hair and makeup people are showing up in half an hour. Eat up and let's get moving. It's time to earn your keep."

"Can't I just take one lick?" Cricket pleads.

She's standing in front of a funky little shave ice shack on Kam Highway, holding a cup of rainbow-colored ice. For the last hour she's been sitting totally still—well, as still as she could manage—while a hair stylist fiddled with her hair and a makeup girl messed with her face.

Now she's trying to remember how excited she felt when she first put on the bathing suit Deirdre gave her—a cute two-piece with red board shorts and a black and white bikini top. But all she can think about is how hot she is, how thirsty she is, and how desperately she needs to scratch her nose.

"No," Deirdre commands. "No licks."

"Why not?"

"Because then we'll have to clean off your mouth and reapply your lip gloss and buy a new shave ice and—"

"Okay, okay!"

"Listen up, Cricket," Josh says, looking through his camera. "I want you to pretend you're just about to take a lick. That's right, but turn your head slightly to the left. Good! Now tilt your chin up a little. Now smile. No, too big. Just a half-smile. Widen your eyes a little . . . and perfect! Don't move!"

Josh snaps a shot, tells Cricket to move six inches to the right, then snaps some more. He keeps snapping until she's ready to run screaming into the highway.

"Don't jiggle your foot," Josh says impatiently. "It's making your head bounce and that's going to put you out of focus."

"I can't help it!" Cricket moans. "This is so boring!"

"Never mind," Deirdre breaks in. "She's got perspiration on her upper lip anyway. Makeup! We need some powder over here!"

"Let's bring Kanani and Isobel into this one," Josh says. "Kanani, sit on the bench. Isobel, you lean against the shave ice shack."

The makeup girl is approaching, brandishing a compact and a makeup brush. Cricket groans. Her throat feels like sandpaper. Impulsively, she shoves her face into the shave ice and bites off a huge chunk. Delicious!

The makeup girl sees her and stops in her tracks. "Deirdre," she calls wearily, "we've got a problem here."

Everyone turns to look at Cricket. Her lips and tongue are stained a bright blue. She shrugs guiltily as a drop of shave ice syrup rolls down her chin. "Sorry," she squeaks.

Deirdre storms over. Suddenly, she looks more like a truant officer than a kindergarten teacher. She grabs Cricket's shoulder—hard!—and snarls, "*Water Woman* has spent a lot of money to bring you girls to Hawaii. All they're asking in return is that you pose for a few pictures. That seems like a pretty good deal, wouldn't you say?"

"Well, sure," Cricket mutters, "but—"

"But nothing! How would you like to be on the next plane home? I can arrange that, young lady."

"No, ma'am."

"Okay. Then let's get cleaned up and try it again." Cricket nods and Deirdre releases her shoulder. "Makeup!" she calls cheerily, as if nothing had happened. "We're ready for you now."

Blushing with embarrassment, Cricket turns to throw her shave ice in the garbage. But Luna's mom intercepts her and gives her a hug. "It's not easy being a supermodel, is it?" she says.

"Stupidmodel is more like it," Cricket answers glumly.

"Relax. Did I ever tell you about the time I was in Maui being photographed for an Ocean Pacific ad? A huge swell had just come through but they wouldn't let me go out. I had to stand on a cliff for hours on end, posing in an OP T-shirt. Finally, we stopped for a ten-minute break and I couldn't stand it anymore. I took off in the rental car and went surfing."

Cricket gasps. "What happened?"

"What do you think? I got fired. But I got some great waves!" Cate chuckles, remembering. "I never did anything that unprofessional again. And I don't want you to, either. I'm just telling you so you know I understand how you feel."

Cricket smiles. She can't believe how cool Cate is. "Thanks," she says gratefully.

Then, with a smile on her face and a whole new attitude, she tosses out her shave ice and turns to face the makeup girl.

Later that night, after everyone has gone to bed, Cricket and Kanani sneak into the kitchen. But they aren't there to raid the refrigerator. They're looking for a phone book.

"Check the drawers," Kanani whispers.

Cricket opens a few drawers but finds only silverware and kitchen utensils. She reaches up to open a cabinet. "Ouch! My back hurts from standing so long in one position, holding that stupid shave ice."

"It was a nightmare," Kanani agrees.

"Oh, here it is," Cricket whispers, pulling a phone book out of the broom closet. She hesitates, then turns to Kanani. "You go first."

Kanani turns on the light. She takes a deep breath and leafs through the pages. Then her hand flies up to her mouth. "He's in here! Liko Kaunolu. Tantalus Drive in Honolulu." Eagerly, she hands the phone book to Cricket. "Now you look up your dad."

With trembling hands, Cricket takes the book and turns to the Cs. There are plenty of Connollys, but no Chet Connolly. A wave of disappointment washes over her, but she forces herself to shrug. "Not here," she says. "But then that's no surprise. He's not the type to have a listed telephone—or any telephone, for that matter."

"Okay, so he's not in the phone book," Kanani replies. "You just have to ask around. If he's on the island, you'll find him sooner or later."

"Yeah, I guess." She pauses. "So are you going to call your dad?"

Kanani looks away. "I . . . I don't know. What if he doesn't want to see me? I don't want to put him in an uncomfortable position."

"Kanani, he's your birthfather! Who cares if he's uncomfortable? You've got a right to see him."

Kanani's face lights up. "Listen, I've got an idea. Let's drive to his house and just . . . I don't know, just scope it out. You know, see where he lives and what he looks like."

A grin creeps up Cricket's face. "You mean, spy on him?"

"Well, I don't know if I'd call it that exactly. Hey, do you think Deirdre would let us borrow the car?"

"Fat chance. But what she doesn't know won't hurt her."

"You mean, just take it without her permission?" Kanani asks anxiously.

Suddenly, Cricket hears footsteps in the hall. She and Kanani freeze as Deirdre appears in the doorway. "What are you girls doing up?" she demands. "Didn't you hear me say we're shooting on the beach at dawn tomorrow?"

"Just getting a drink," Cricket says as the girls hurry past her and into their bedroom. "Good night, Deirdre."

As they hop into bed, Kanani turns to Cricket and whispers, "Tomorrow night—let's do it!"

4

Good. Very good," Josh says, prowling around the girls with his camera in his hands. "Now move a little closer together. Okay, look at me. That's it! Now, smile!"

Cricket and the girls are kneeling side by side at the water's edge. Gritting her teeth, Cricket tries to ignore the wet sand that's grinding into her knees. Instead, she concentrates on the gorgeous red, white, and blue bikini she's wearing.

"That looks more like a grimace than a smile, Cricket," Josh scolds. "Now, come on. Give me all you've got."

What I've got is a desperate need to go surfing, Cricket thinks. But she forces a smile as Josh snaps a series of shots.

"Oh, yeah!" he exclaims as he clicks the shutter. "Fantastic! Beautiful!"

Deirdre stands behind him, nodding her approval. Then suddenly, she looks over the girls' heads and her expression turns to alarm. Cricket, noticing Deirdre's widening eyes and gaping mouth, spins around to see what she's looking at.

Just as she does, a wave—twice as big as anything that's hit the beach all morning—whacks her right in the face! She screams and tumbles backward, falling on her friends, who are also screaming and flailing around.

They land in a tangle, sandy and soaked, as the broken wave recedes. "Ew!" Rae moans. "I've got sand in my bathing suit!"

"I've got sand in my teeth!" Cricket wails, spitting repeatedly.

"Everybody up!" Deirdre shouts. "Have a drink. Get dried off. Then we'll redo your hair and makeup and start over."

The girls let out a collective groan. "We're tired!" Luna cries.

"Yeah." Cricket nods. "We've been at this for three hours. When can we catch some waves?"

"I'll take you surfing this afternoon," Cate pipes up.

"Hurray!" the girls shout, slapping high fives and tapping fists.

Cricket grabs her towel and dries off. Then she takes a Coke from the cooler and swishes the sweet, cold, fizzy liquid over her gritty teeth. The other girls reach for their own drinks and sprawl beside her in the sand.

"Gee, that was fun," Luna says sarcastically.

"I thought modeling was going to be easy," Cricket declares. "You put on a bathing suit, you stand there. Nothing to it." She shakes her head. "Just shows how wrong you can be."

"Really," Kanani agrees. "It's uncomfortable, it's boring, it's—"

"But wait till you see how fabulous you look in the magazine," a voice says.

The girls look up as Suzie Goldberg walks across the beach to join them. "Hi," she says. "I came by to see how things are going."

"We just got drenched by a rogue wave," Cricket tells her.

"Cricket's still trying to get the sand out of her teeth," Isobel adds.

Suzie cracks up, and soon her infectious laugher has them all giggling.

"I hope Josh snapped a shot of the wave whacking you in the head," Suzie chuckles. "We'll put it in the next issue with the caption '*You, too, can be a glamorous surf model!*' That should get the young girls lining up to try surfing, don't you think?"

Everyone is laughing so hard, they almost forget how tired they are. Suzie walks over to take a Capri-Sun from the cooler. Suddenly, Cricket has an idea.

"Suzie," she asks, jogging over to join her, "how long have you lived on Oahu?"

"All my life," she answers.

Cricket silently kicks herself for thinking Suzie's blond hair and white skin mean she's not a local. Hawaii, she's learning, is full of surprises. "Then you must know a lot of people—especially surfers."

"Oh, yeah. Growing up here—plus writing for *Water Woman*—I know practically all the locals and most of the regulars who come here for the winter."

"Do you know Chet Connolly?" Cricket asks.

"Amazing surfer, that guy. He comes to the North Shore every season. Kind of keeps to himself, though. Doesn't party or hang out in town. I've met him, but I can't say I really know him. Why?"

Cricket hesitates. "He . . . he's my father," she says.

Suzie looks at her with new interest. "No kidding? No wonder you're such a good surfer. You've got the genes, girl."

The compliment makes Cricket stand a little taller. Then she realizes Suzie hasn't seen her surf yet. Her shoulders fall. "Do you know where he's staying?" she asks.

Suzie shakes her head. "Haven't seen him yet this winter. He usually stays with friends, but I'm not sure where. I think he moves around a lot." She pauses. "You don't have his number?"

Cricket shrugs. "Like you said, he kind of keeps to himself."

Suzie doesn't probe any further. "I'll ask around, see if I can find out anything. Okay?"

Cricket nods gratefully. "Thanks, Suzie." She gulps down the last of her Coke and turns away.

If Dad's here, she thinks, *I'll bet Suzie will track him down.* The thought excites her and scares her. Will her father want to see her? Only time will tell.

That afternoon, Cate takes the girls surfing at Kammieland, a break that lies across the channel from Sunset Beach. The surf is a solid six to eight feet, with powerful lefts and rights that keep the girls' hearts pumping—especially when they look down and see the shallow coral reef beneath them.

But the girls' biggest challenge isn't the amping surf or the jagged reef. It's the crowds. The break is packed with surfers—locals, visitors, even a couple of famous faces the girls recognize from the surf magazines.

As each wave rolls in, everyone jockeys for position, but only one can claim the plum spot in the pocket. That means the losers have to pull out fast. If they don't, they get thrown over the falls or plowed into by another surfer.

"That was harsh," Cricket pants as they sit on the beach afterward. "I only got two waves."

"But they were juicy," Luna points out. "Your backside snaps were all-time."

Cricket grins. "How about that tube you got? You disappeared for like five seconds!"

Kanani plops down next to Cricket. "I only got one wave," she complains. "And that was because nobody else wanted it."

"You've got to be more aggressive," Rae says, towel-drying her short, strawberry-blond hair. "Those surfers out there are no better than you. Don't let them intimidate you."

Kanani snorts a laugh. "Veronica Kay is no better than me?" she asks, naming one of the pros who was in the lineup. "I wish!"

"Don't be so hard on yourselves," Cate breaks in. "Remember, this is only your second North Shore session." She stands up and adds, "What you girls need is some food. Let's drive into Haleiwa for dinner."

"I've got a pounding headache," Kanani says, nudging Cricket. "Do you mind dropping me at the house? I'll grab something from the fridge."

Cricket turns to her friend. Then she catches Kanani's meaningful glance and suddenly she understands—Kanani wants to borrow the other Xterra and drive to her father's house tonight. "Can I go home, too?" she asks Cate. "I'm wiped out."

Cate looks at them with bewilderment. "I hope you two aren't coming down with a cold or something." Then she shrugs and says, "Get some rest. We'll bring you home a dessert from Sunset Sensations."

An hour later, Kanani is driving the yellow Xterra into the hills high above Honolulu. Cricket sits beside her, gripping the armrest as Kanani steers around a series of nerve-racking hairpin turns.

"I can't believe we're only a few miles from downtown," Cricket remarks as they drive past a thick forest of bamboo. "It feels like we're in the middle of a jungle or something."

"What I can't believe is that anyone actually lives up here," Kanani replies. "Have you seen any houses?"

"I think I saw a roof back there, but it was below the road. Maybe I'm hallucinating."

"Well, it *is* pretty hilly up here. According to the map, we're in the foothills of the Koolau mountain range."

"Look, there's a driveway," Cricket announces. "Check the number on the mailbox."

"Hey, we're getting close," Kanani says. Suddenly, she slams on the brakes as a furry brown animal darts across the road. "What the heck was that?" she gasps.

"A mongoose!" Cricket exclaims. "I saw one by the palm trees behind our house the other night."

The mongoose reminds her of Kainoa. She pictures his handsome face and his long, flowing hair. Will she ever see him again? Then she remembers how he cut her off in the surf and laughed about it. *Forget it*, she thinks. *If I never see him again it will be too soon.*

Kanani takes a deep breath and they drive on, past towering banyan trees and thick, green rain forest.

"There it is!" Cricket cries. "Turn off! Turn off!"

Kanani veers down a steep, winding driveway. They drive down, down until finally they catch a glimpse of rooftop. Kanani pulls over and turns off the car. "We'd better walk the rest of the way," she says.

The air is filled with a damp, earthy smell. Colorful birds flit through the treetops. The girls walk down the driveway, keeping an eye out for people.

"All this sneaking around feels weird," Cricket whispers. "I mean, what if someone sees us and calls the cops? We could get arrested for trespassing."

"It'll be fine," Kanani replies, but she doesn't look very confident. She's biting her lip and there's a frown on her pretty face.

The girls round a bend and suddenly they're standing in front of an elegant pink house with a red tile roof and a breathtaking view of the city and the ocean below.

"Whoa!" Cricket breathes. "This place is practically a mansion."

Kanani nods and moves closer. With Cricket by her side, she edges up to one of the windows and peeks inside. Suddenly, she lets out a little gasp.

"What is it?" Cricket asks, leaning around her friend to take a look. One glimpse and her jaw drops. She's looking into a casually elegant living room with tile floors, colorful area rugs, and beautiful watercolor paintings on the walls. Beyond it she can see into the dining room where a middle-aged couple is eating dinner around a glass-topped table.

Cricket leans closer. The man is wearing tan slacks and an expensive-looking Hawaiian shirt. His dark face is ruggedly handsome and his thick hair is gray at the temples. The woman is wearing a floor-length

Hawaiian-print dress. Her long, black hair is arranged in a bun. Both of them look elegant, sophisticated, and very rich.

"I . . . I always imagined my birthfather was a famous surfer," Kanani says, half to herself. "But that guy looks like a businessman or something."

Cricket nods. "Somehow I can't picture him with a surfboard under his arm."

Kanani lets out a sigh. "Let's go."

"That's it? You aren't going to talk to him?"

"What would I say to someone like that?"

"How about, 'Hi, Dad. I'm your daughter,'" Cricket suggests.

Kanani shakes her head. "I couldn't. I'd be too intimidated. Besides, if he wanted to meet me, he would have contacted me by now. He's probably trying to forget I even exist."

"You don't know that," Cricket begins. "Besides—"

But Kanani is already heading back to the car. Cricket follows, her thoughts turning to her own father. Will she find him? And if she does, how will he react? Sure, he sent her some homemade surf wax, but that doesn't necessarily mean he wants to meet her— let alone start a real relationship.

Maybe Kanani has the right idea, she tells herself. Better to scope out the situation first, then decide if she wants to contact her dad.

But first, she reminds herself, *I have to find him.*

5

"You girls need to learn that your actions have consequences," Cate says sternly. "The rest of us are going snorkeling, but not you two. I want you to stay home and think about what you did."

Cricket and Kanani stand in the driveway, watching dejectedly as Cate, Deirdre, Josh, and the other girls climb into the Xterras and drive away.

"Oh, man, this sucks," Kanani moans, trudging back into the house.

"If only we had gotten home ten minutes earlier," Cricket declares, "they never would have known we were gone."

"I've never seen Cate so pissed," Kanani says. "Even when we were in Florida, and Rae and I sneaked off during a hurricane."

"Maybe we should have told her the truth about where we were last night," Cricket says.

Kanani shakes her head. "And have everyone grill me about my birthfather? The girls all think he's some Hawaiian surf god. I can't face telling them the truth."

"But what is the truth?" Cricket asks. "You don't even know what your birthfather does for a living. All you know is he's got a nice house in the Honolulu hills."

"Well, he's not a surfer, that's for sure. He's probably some rich corporate type who only cares about making money."

Cricket flops down on the sofa and lets out a sigh. "I thought Cate would understand if I said we borrowed the Xterra to go surfing. After all, that's what she did when she was in Maui shooting that OP ad."

"That trick never works. My uncle once told me that my mom flunked chemistry when she was in high school. Then I brought home a C and she grounded me for a month. Go figure."

"Parents!" Cricket says with disgust, forgetting that just yesterday she thought Cate was the coolest mom in the world.

"I'm going into the bedroom to write in my journal," Kanani says with a sigh.

Cricket nods. She probably should do the same, but sitting still just isn't her style. Instead, she grabs a Coke from the fridge and a bag of Oreos from the cabinet. She wanders back and forth from the kitchen to the living room, gulping, munching, and stressing.

Finally, she can't stand it anymore. She hates being

cooped up inside! Walking out to the lanai, she gazes longingly at the white sand and the sparkling blue ocean.

Cate said I should stay in the house and think about what I did, she reminds herself. But she always thinks much better when she's moving. So why not take a walk on the beach? She'll make sure she's back long before Cate and the gang return.

Cricket hops off the lanai and jogs down to the beach. Left will take her to Lili'u's Reef; right to . . . who knows where? She decides to go right. With the sun on her shoulders and the water lapping at her feet, she feels her spirits rise. She's in Hawaii, on the famous North Shore. It's a dream come true!

In the distance, she sees a man with long, dark hair approaching. Her heart leaps into her throat. Could it be Kainoa? But as he comes closer, she sees it isn't. Instantly, her heart sinks back into her chest.

Why do I care? she wonders. Sure, she likes Kainoa's dark eyes, his handsome face, his flowing hair. And that body! Some girls might think he's too skinny, but not Cricket. She likes his narrow hips, his flat stomach, and his long, long legs.

But what good is a handsome face if it's combined with a lousy personality? Cricket asks herself.

That night on the beach, Kainoa had been alternately flirtatious and slightly condescending. But that was nothing compared to the way he acted out in the water. The shock and disappointment she felt when he paddled past her still stung. And then, when he dropped in on her—and laughed about it! That was beyond rude!

So why do I keep thinking about him? Cricket wonders.

Maybe it has something to do with what Suzie Goldberg said—about how Lili'u's Reef is a locals' beach, and how the popular surf breaks on the North Shore are overcrowded because of all the visiting surfers. Well, she saw that yesterday. Kammieland was packed, and Sunset was a total zoo.

Is that why Kainoa was so unfriendly? Cricket longs to ask him. She wants to understand. But how can she do either when he won't even acknowledge her presence?

And then her thoughts turn to her father. She was only five when he moved out and, over the years, he's barely acknowledged her presence, either. Oh, sure, he's sent an occasional birthday or Christmas present, but usually they were much too young for her or totally inappropriate—like on her eighth birthday when he sent her a video of *Big Wednesday,* a surfing movie that was way over her head.

So why can't she stop thinking about him? And why has she spent the last six months trying to find him? Maybe it's because lately she's gotten serious about her surfing. That means she and her father have something in common now. Something to share. And maybe—just maybe—he'll finally want her around.

The birthday gift of the surf wax seemed to confirm

that. For once her dad had given her something she really wanted. Plus, it implied he was paying attention to her and knew her surfing was improving.

But then why didn't he deliver the surf wax in person? Or at least include his phone number and return address? Cricket doesn't know. In fact, there's only one thing she knows for sure. When she thinks of her dad, she feels an aching emptiness inside—an emptiness that can only be filled by her father's love.

Cricket lets out a shaky sigh and walks on. Up ahead, she sees some waves peeling off a jagged rock about twenty-five yards offshore. There are only three surfers out and—wonder of wonders!—they seem to be taking turns catching the waves instead of jockeying madly, trying to cut off the others.

Cricket stops to watch. All three surfers are longboarders. One of them takes off and walks to the nose. *Too bad Kanani isn't here,* Cricket thinks. Kanani is a longboarder who favors soul-surfing over competition. It's obvious these guys feel the same way.

A second surfer paddles into a wave. He pops up and leans forward into a unique and graceful crouch. Cricket gasps. She knows that stance! She's seen it in dozens of surfing books and magazines. It belongs to Chet "The Panther" Connolly—her father!

But can it really be him? Cricket wades into the shallow water to get a better look. The surfer cuts left and then glides down the line. As he surfs toward the shore, Cricket studies his deep-set eyes, his long, slender nose, the cleft in his chin. He looks just like the father she remembers, except with more wrinkles and grayer hair.

Cricket has a sudden desire to call out to him. She pictures him paddling toward her with a big smile on his face, then throwing his arms around her and pulling her close. But what if it isn't him? She'll look like a complete fool, calling "Dad!" to a total stranger.

Then Cricket has an inspiration. She'll run back to the house and get her surfboard. Then she'll paddle out and show her dad she's grown up into the daughter he's always wanted—a surfer girl who knows how to rip. She pictures him nodding approvingly as she carves across the wave. Just the thought of it gives her a warm feeling inside.

And if the guy isn't her dad? He'll never know what she was thinking. And at least she'll catch a few waves, which means the morning won't be a total loss.

Suddenly, a horrible thought occurs to Cricket. What if the guy leaves before she gets back? She can't let that happen! She turns and sprints up the beach like an Olympian, making it back to the house in record time. As she grabs her board off the lanai, Kanani appears at the door.

"Where have you been?" she asks with a worried frown. "If Cate and the others get back and find you gone, you'll be in major trouble!"

"This is more important than Cate," Cricket pants. "It's more important than anything."

"What is it? What's going on?"

"I'll tell you later," she says, dashing across the burning sand.

She runs back to the break. The surfers are still there! With her heart pounding and her breath coming in jagged gasps, she jumps in the water. It's only then that she realizes she's wearing shorts and a halter top, not a bathing suit. But it's too late to worry about that now. Quickly, she hops on her board and paddles out.

She's halfway out to the lineup when her father—or at least the man she *thinks* is her father—takes off on a wave. As he surfs toward her, she stops paddling and sits up on her board. He notices her and glances over. Then, like a character in a brainless TV sitcom, he does a double take. His eyes widen, his jaw drops, and— boom!—he loses his balance and wipes out.

Cricket can't help but laugh. But her laughter dies in her throat as the guy pops to the surface, retrieves his board, and paddles toward the shore as if the devil were on his tail. Cricket watches, stunned. Why isn't he coming over? It's like he doesn't want to talk to her or even look at her. It's like he's running away.

Tears well up in Cricket's eyes. It feels like the empty space inside her is growing bigger—so big it threatens to consume her entire being. But then another feeling emerges. Anger! It's one thing for her father to ignore her when she's in Crescent Cove and he's who-knows-where. But to have him ignore her when she's sitting right in front of him—that's just too much!

Then and there, Cricket decides she has to know the truth. Is this man her father? And if so, why won't he talk to her? Why is he acting like an escaped convict who just caught sight of the cops?

Cricket throws herself down on her surfboard and paddles after her father with all her might. She reaches the shore and looks around. There he is, his board balanced on his head, striding quickly toward the parking lot.

Tossing aside her surfboard, she runs after him. She catches up to him just as he throws his board in the back of an old black pickup truck and starts to climb inside.

"Wait!" she cries, grabbing his arm.

He stops and stares at her. As their identical steel-gray eyes meet, she knows the truth. She's found her dad.

6

Dad," Cricket blurts out, "it's me, Cricket."

"I know," he says as if he'd spent the last ten years reading her bedtime stories and helping her with her homework instead of being completely out of touch. "Did you like the surf wax I sent you for your birthday?"

The question throws her off balance and all the things she planned to ask fly out of her head. "Uh . . . yeah," she answers. "Actually, it was the best wax I've ever used."

"You know, most surfers think all surf wax is the same, but they're wrong," he says, his rapid-fire speech sounding to Cricket amazingly like her own way of speaking. "I've been trying for years to come up with the perfect combination of ingredients."

"Really?" she asks. "What are they?"

"Did you know there was a time when surfers didn't even use wax?" her father asks, ignoring her question.

"To create traction, surfboard shapers used to sprinkle sand across the varnish when it was still wet. That gritty finish would scrape your skin right off!"

He laughs and it sounds like a lower-pitched version of her own laugh. "Yeah," he continues, "Arthur Gallant Jr. was the first surfer to wax his board back in 1935. His mom had just waxed the floor and he noticed how his feet practically stuck to the wood when he walked across it. So he poured some floor wax on his board. But floor wax was expensive then, so his mom gave him a bar of paraffin instead. It worked great!"

Cricket is getting totally sucked into her father's story. She loves surf history, she loves science, and she adores the combination of the two. That's why she spends every morning checking the Internet surf reports, trying to understand how weather affects the waves. The other girls think it's totally boring—they just want to know *where* the waves are breaking, not *why*—but Cricket finds it fascinating.

"Paraffin was used for the next thirty or so years," her father explains. "Then in the fifties and sixties, guys started melting it down and experimenting with it, trying to come up with a product specifically for surfers. There was Mike Doyle's Waxmate, Fred Herzog's Mr. Zog's Sex Wax, Sticky Bumps from Wax Research . . . but mine is better than all of 'em."

"What do you use?" Cricket asks curiously.

"It's a combination of soybean wax, beeswax, and—wait a minute! Those ingredients are top secret!"

His words remind Cricket of what she really wants to say to her father. "That's so like you!" she blurts out. "You don't let me in on anything in your life. Why would I think you'd tell me what's in your stupid surf wax?"

Her father's mouth opens and closes, but nothing comes out. Cricket barely notices, however, because she's too angry to see straight. "Why did you walk out on Mom and me?" she demands. "Why haven't you come to see me, or e-mailed me, or even called? Why have you been spying on me like some wacko stalker? And why did you ignore me out in the surf just now?"

"Because I knew you were going to ask me a lot of hard questions," he says, looking down at his feet. "I was right, too."

"Yeah, well, why don't you answer them?"

"It's hard to explain," he mutters. "Some people just . . . that is, I'm not one of those guys . . . I mean, it's like those old cowboy movies . . ." His voice trails off and he shrugs—once, twice, three times.

Cricket stares at him, uncomprehending.

"Look," he says, climbing into the front seat of his truck, "be here tomorrow at sunrise. Bring your board."

"What?" she stammers. "Tomorrow? But—"

He slams the truck door, cutting off her words. Then he slips his key in the ignition and starts the engine.

"Dad!" she calls. "Wait! Don't go!"

He mouths the word *tomorrow,* then backs up and

drives out of the parking lot, sending up a cloud of dust behind him.

Cricket stands there, staring after him until his truck disappears behind a line of palm trees. There are so many emotions ricocheting around inside her—anger, frustration, confusion, excitement—that she feels light-headed. All she knows for certain is she can't wait until tomorrow!

"Where were you?" Kanani cries, flinging open the back door as Cricket walks onto the lanai. "I was going out of my mind!"

Cricket leans her surfboard against the wall and turns to her friend. "I found my father."

"What? Oh, my God, Cricket! Where?"

"Out in the water. He was surfing. That's why I came back to get my board."

"Did you talk to him?" Kanani asks eagerly.

"Sort of. He told me about the history of surf wax."

Kanani stares at her in disbelief. "Surf wax?"

She nods. "And he said to meet him on the beach tomorrow at sunrise. He said to bring my board."

"Cricket, that's awesome!" Kanani exclaims.

"Yeah, I guess."

Kanani frowns. "What's wrong?"

"I suppose I feel a little like you did when you saw your birthfather. Not that my dad is wealthy and sophisticated or anything," she adds quickly. "It's just . . . I don't know, Kanani. I'm not sure he really wants to get to know me."

"He sent you that surf wax, didn't he? And he told you to meet him tomorrow morning."

"Yeah. But what if he doesn't like me? What if I don't like him?"

"You'll never know if you don't take the first step."

"That's what I told you when we were at your birth-father's house," Cricket reminds her.

"That's different," Kanani says, turning away. "My dad's not a surfer. Besides, if he really cares about me, why did he let my birthmother put me up for adoption?"

Cricket doesn't know the answer. She wants to say something reassuring, but just then the front door bursts open and Luna calls, "Anybody home?"

The girls hurry in from the lanai. "How was it?" Kanani asks.

"Magical!" Luna cries, tossing her backpack down on a chair.

"You can't believe what's down there under the surface of the water," Rae exclaims. "It's like the world's biggest tropical aquarium."

Deirdre and Josh walk in and head for their bedrooms. Cate is still outside, unloading things from the car.

"Cate had this waterproof identification card with her," Isobel says, heading to the fridge for a bottle of water. "I swear we must have seen three-quarters of the fish on it."

"And not just fish!" Luna exclaims. "We even saw a moray eel."

Isobel shivers. "That thing gave me the creeps!"

"And a whitetip reef shark," Luna continues.

"A shark!" Kanani cries.

"They don't attack humans," Rae explains. "In fact, Cate says you can swim right up to them."

"Deirdre wouldn't let us, though," Luna says. "I guess she thought her models wouldn't look as good with a couple of bloody chunks taken out of them."

The girls laugh as Deirdre walks in from the hallway. "Don't get too comfortable, girls. We're heading out again in a couple of minutes."

"Where?" Kanani asks eagerly. It's obvious she's dying to get out of the house. Cricket, however, keeps quiet. After the stress of meeting her father, she's ready for a nap.

"We have a photo session at Kapena this afternoon," Deirdre explains.

"Is that a waterfall?" Luna asks.

"Just wait till you see," her mother says, walking in with a cooler and a pile of wet towels in her arms. "It's gorgeous."

"But what about lunch?" Rae asks.

"We'll take some sandwiches and have a picnic by the swimming hole," Deirdre says. "Now let's hop to it. I told the makeup girl and the hair stylist we'd be there by noon."

"Hey, isn't this near where your birthdad lives?" Cricket whispers to Kanani as Cate drives the red Xterra onto Pali Highway.

Cate confirms it when she points out the window at a craggy green mountaintop and says, "That's Tantalus Peak. In Greek mythology, Tantalus was the son of Zeus. He was invited to eat with the gods, but when he shared the ambrosia with some mortals, the gods punished him by forcing him to stand in a pool of water up to his chin. When he tried to drink, the water was always just out of grasp. Fruit hung over his head, but when he tried to eat, he couldn't reach it."

"I feel his pain," Rae says from the front seat. "Did you see those delicious-looking sandwiches Deirdre made? I tried to grab one before we left, but she said we couldn't eat until we got to the falls."

"That's why she put the food in her car," Cate laughs. "She knew you'd raid the cooler."

"I'm hungry. So shoot me."

"We'll be there soon," Cate says reassuringly.

Cricket notices a newspaper stuffed between the front seats. Eager to soak up a little island ambience— and maybe check out the surf report—she picks it up.

"How can you read when we're going around all these curves?" Kanani asks.

Cricket shrugs. She never gets carsick. She opens the

paper and leafs through it. An editorial criticizing real estate development around Velzyland catches her eye. According to the editorial, the new buildings will block beach access except at one narrow point.

Suddenly, Cricket hears Kanani gasp. Looking up, she sees her friend staring at the newspaper in total shock. "What?" Cricket asks.

Kanani points to a list of names at the top of the editorial page. Cricket reads it and her eyes widen. *Liko Kaunolu, Executive Editor.*

Kanani's birthfather is the editor of the *Oahu Daily News!*

7

*H*ere we are," Cate says, pulling over at a scenic over-look along Pali Highway.

Deirdre, in the yellow Xterra, coasts up beside them. They all pile out of the car and start unloading coolers, towels, and a box of brand-new bathing suits. A minute later, the hair stylist and the makeup girl turn off the highway and park beside them.

"Okay, according to my information, it's this way," Deirdre says, lifting the box of bikinis into her arms.

Soon they're all stumbling down a steep, muddy trail. "Hey, look," Luna says, pointing to a rock wall enclosed with protective grating.

They step closer. There's a carving on the wall of a man and a dog.

"It's a petroglyph," Cate explains. "Artwork done by ancient Hawaiians."

"Whoa!" Cricket breathes. "It's so cool to think of

someone thousands of years ago standing right here where we are now."

She turns to Kanani, who she knows is fascinated by all things Hawaiian. But her friend is staring off into the middle distance. *She's probably thinking about her birthfather*, Cricket realizes.

"Why are there flowers and leis all around the rock?" Luna asks.

"People must leave them as an offering of some kind," Cate replies. "I don't know the history."

They continue on, climbing over rocks and hopping over patches of mud. At one point, Deirdre slips and falls on her rear end. To Cricket's amazement, she manages to hold on to the box of bathing suits.

Cricket looks at Deirdre, sitting in a patch of mud with a startled look on her face. It's all Cricket can do not to laugh. Then she glances at Luna and completely loses it. The two dissolve into a fit of giggles. Soon everyone else joins in—everyone except Deirdre, that is.

"I could have regained my balance if it wasn't for this stupid box," she declares. As they walk on, she mutters, "Somebody's got to make sure this fashion shoot is a success. If it wasn't for me, nothing would ever get done."

"Ooh, aren't we important?" Cricket whispers to Kanani.

But Kanani's mind is still on her birthdad. "Executive editor of the biggest newspaper on the island," she says. "That's a really important job."

Before Cricket can answer, they turn the corner and catch their first glimpse of Kapena Falls. "Wow!" Cricket exclaims.

The waterfall begins its descent high up on a rock wall—almost as high as the roof of a two-story building, Cricket estimates. Then it cascades down the rocks and splashes into a wide pool surrounded by lush jungle.

"Check it out!" Isobel says. On one side of the pool, some local kids are swinging on a rope that's been tied to a banyan tree. Shrieking and giggling, they fly out over the water and land with a splash.

"I want to try it," Cricket says eagerly.

"Not yet," Deirdre breaks in. "You can't get wet until we get our photos."

Cate opens the cooler. Cricket is expecting a relaxing little picnic, but instead Deirdre makes the girls gulp their finger sandwiches while the hair stylist works on their hair. Then they have to sit still even longer while the makeup girl works on their faces.

Finally, they're ready to put on the bathing suits. Deirdre and Josh have set up a small tent at the edge of the pool. The girls crawl in, change their clothes, and crawl out. Cricket looks down admiringly at the maroon plaid bikini Deirdre has chosen for her. *This bikini is hot! I just love it!*

Josh takes a few photos of them standing by the pool while the local kids point and giggle. Next, he has the girls wade into the water as he snaps some more.

Finally, he instructs them to stand next to the water-fall. Cricket sighs. She's so hot and sweaty! If only he'd let them jump in!

"Okay, Cricket," Josh calls, "cup your hands and put them into the waterfall, like you're going to take a drink."

Cricket does as she's told, but after the fifth photograph, she can't stand it anymore. Accidentally on purpose, she leans a little too close to the tumbling water. It splashes onto her face and sprays her hair.

"Oh, Cricket!" Josh moans. "That's it, you're finished. Luna, you're next. Get over there."

"Whoopee!" Cricket exclaims, diving into the cool water. She gets to her feet and pushes her wet hair back from her forehead.

Luna gazes at her enviously. Leaning down, she splashes water at Cricket's face. Without thinking, Cricket splashes back.

"No!" Deirdre wails. "You have to stay dry until—"

But it's too late. All the girls are joining in, splashing each other and giggling like a bunch of kindergartners.

"Stop!" Deirdre orders. "Stop it, I said!"

"Shut up, Deirdre," Josh calls, snapping photo after photo. "I'm getting some great stuff here!"

Deirdre lets out a melodramatic sigh and throws up her hands. "Whatever," she says.

The girls splash over to the rope swing. Joining the little kids, they take turns swinging out over the pool and leaping into the water. Josh hovers around them, snapping photos, while Deirdre and Cate look on from a shady spot on the shore.

Cricket is waiting her turn for the rope swing when she notices two people step out of the jungle at the top of the falls. Shading her eyes against the sun, she gazes up at them. They're teenage boys with nut-brown skin—Hawaiian locals, she figures.

Then a third boy emerges from the foliage and takes his place on the rocky ledge. Cricket's breath catches in her throat. The boy is tall and thin, with long, wavy black hair. Can it be? Yes, it's Kainoa!

This time Cricket isn't going to wave and risk rejection. No, she decides, she'll just keep an eye on him and see if he notices her. As she watches, he jokes with his friends. She can see them laughing and nudging each other. Then Kainoa steps to the edge of the rocks and lifts his arms high over his head.

Cricket freezes. It looks like he's going to jump! But no, it can't be. It's much too high, and the pool isn't deep enough. He'll crack his head open!

And he doesn't jump—he *dives*! A small, strangled cry escapes from Cricket's lips. Kanani and Rae, who are standing beside her in line, turn to see what's going on. When they spot Kainoa, they stop and stare.

Kainoa does a picture-perfect swan dive and hits the water right in front of the falls. He lands so perfectly there's barely a ripple. Cricket holds her breath, waiting for him to surface. He appears a moment later, bursting out of the water like a phoenix rising from the ashes.

Kanani and Rae, not realizing that Kainoa is the same boy who dropped in on Cricket at Lili'u's Reef, burst into wild applause. Kainoa glances over at them. At the same moment, the little kid in front of Cricket grabs the rope and swings across the water. Now it's Cricket's turn.

Oh, no! she thinks. *He's looking right at me.*

She hesitates, but Rae gives her a friendly shove. "Go on. It's your turn."

Cricket scrambles onto the roots of the banyan tree and grabs the rope. She leaps into space and soars out over the pool. Determined not to look like a fool in front of Kainoa, she releases the rope at its highest point and tucks into a cannonball, hitting the water with an enormous splash.

As she pops up, she sees Kainoa grinning and clapping. "Good job, haole girl. I think you're ready to try the falls, yeah?"

"Are you crazy?" she says. "Jump from up there?"

"It's perfectly safe as long as you know what you're doing. I'll teach you how." He pauses. "Unless you're too scared, that is."

No way is Cricket going to let anyone accuse her of being chicken—especially not this infuriating, condescending local boy! "I'm not scared," she declares.

"Then follow me." Kainoa begins climbing up the craggy rock wall, looking for all the world like a Hawaiian Spider-Man. "Put your hands and feet exactly where I put mine," he says over his shoulder.

Cricket takes a deep breath. Then she starts up the

rocks. Quickly, she discovers there are fairly obvious handholds and footholds. Carefully, she mirrors Kainoa's movements and works her way up the rock face.

Beneath her, she hears Deirdre calling, "Cricket, get down from there this minute! The magazine isn't going to pay your medical bills if you get hurt."

Cricket rolls her eyes. Deirdre doesn't care about anything except getting the job done. *Does she ever do anything just because it's fun?* she wonders. It's hard to imagine.

"Be careful, Cricket," Cate calls. "Don't do anything stupid."

Cate's warning hits her a lot harder than Deirdre's. She hesitates, wondering if she's making a big mistake. Just then, Kainoa scrambles over the top of the ledge and holds out his hand. She takes it and he pulls her up beside him.

The two other guys eye her warily. "Cricket, these are my bruddahs, Manu and Palani," Kainoa says.

"Brothers? But you all look the same age."

The boys break into laughter. "*Bruddahs* means 'buddies' in pidgin," Kainoa explains.

"What's pidgin?" she asks, more confused by the second.

"Local slang. It's what we talk when we don't want you haoles to understand us."

"Oh."

Manu and Palani walk to the edge of the rock and

dive off, one by one. Now Cricket and Kainoa are alone at the top of the waterfall.

"Since you're a beginner, you should jump, not dive," he says. "See where the boys jumped? Stand right there and aim for a spot just in front of the falls. The water is deep—maybe twenty feet, thirty feet."

Cricket walks to the edge of the rocks and looks down. Yikes! The water seems so far away! "I—I don't know if I can do it," she stammers.

"Sure you can. You're one brave haole girl. Didn't you surf Lili'u's Reef even though the bruddahs cut you off? I saw you wipe out and come back for more."

She steps back from the edge and turns to face him. "I've been wanting to ask you about that. Why were those guys so mean to us? And why did you ignore me? You could have introduced me to your friends and made things a little easier for me and my crew. Instead, you dropped in on me. What's up with that?"

"Hey, I wanted to talk to you," Kainoa says with a shrug, "but the bruddahs wouldn't have understood. Lili'u's Reef is a local beach. You want to surf the North Shore, you should go to one of the famous spots with all the other haoles."

"Lili'u's Reef is North Shore, too," Cricket shoots back. She puts her hands on her hips. "You know, I don't get you. If you came to Crescent Cove, I'd welcome you into the lineup. I wouldn't hassle you the way your friends hassled me."

"Once upon a time," Kainoa says, "this was our island. But the haoles took it from us. Now they think it's theirs—just a tropical theme park to use however they want. But what about us—the kamaaina, the native Hawaiians? We gotta save a little bit of paradise for ourselves, right?"

Cricket frowns, trying to understand.

"A long time ago," he continues, "there was a family who lived above Kapena Falls. They owned five dogs. The dogs barked at people who passed, but never harmed them. Then one day, some friends of the family were on their way to the falls. The dogs growled and blocked their path, so finally the people turned back. Later, they found out there had been robbers at the falls, attacking everyone who came there. Then the people knew the truth—the dogs were *kupuas*—ghost dogs. Ever since, visitors to the falls leave offerings for the kupuas to thank them for their help."

"That must be why we saw all those flowers and leis on the rock," Cricket says.

Kainoa takes a step toward her. "Are you a robber who's come to the island to steal from the kamaaina? Or are you a pretty girl who's come here to steal my heart?"

Cricket stares at him, too stunned to speak. Did she just hear what she thought she heard?

"Come on," he says suddenly, grabbing her hand and pulling her toward the edge. "We'll jump together."

"Wait!" she cries, but he ignores her and leaps off the rocks, dragging her with him.

Screaming, they plummet through the air and land with a splash at the base of the waterfall. He's still holding her hand as they swim toward the surface.

"I did it!" she shouts, bursting out of the water. "I did it!"

Cricket's friends are clapping and cheering, but she sees only Kainoa. He grins and squeezes her hand. "Like I told you, you're one brave haole girl. And you're right—you do know how to surf. I saw you at Kammieland the other day. The truth is, Cricket, you rip."

8

It's still dark when Cricket climbs out of bed and slips silently into her bathing suit. She glances at Kanani to make sure she's still asleep. Then she tiptoes down the hall and steps quietly out onto the lanai.

A gibbous moon is shining, but above the horizon, the sky is slowly turning from black to gray. The sweet scent of flowers is in the air. With her heart skittering against her ribs, Cricket grabs her board and power-walks up the beach to meet her father.

What will she find when she gets there? Will her dad give her another rambling lecture about surf wax? Or will he sit her down and explain why he walked out ten years ago and never came back? Cricket doesn't know. All she knows is that something deep inside her is drawing her back to him. They were meant to be together again. She just knows it.

Up ahead she sees the spot where her father was

surfing yesterday. She breaks into a run, trying to ignore the butterflies in her stomach. But when she gets there, there's nobody in the water. The beach is deserted, and the parking lot is empty, too.

Cricket feels like she just showed up for her very first pro contest, only to find it's been canceled. The disappointment is so intense, she can feel it in the pit of her stomach.

But it's still early, she reminds herself. Anyway, she's here at the beach with her board under her arm. She might as well go out. So she waxes up and paddles into the peeling four-foot surf.

The sky above the palm trees is beginning to turn soft pink as she takes off on her first wave. And then she sees her father's black pickup truck pulling into the parking lot. Her heart lifts and she starts waving wildly. Almost instantly, she loses her balance and wipes out.

How embarrassing! With luck, her father didn't see that. She scrambles back on her board as he walks down to the water. As she watches him, it's obvious why people call him "the Panther." Chet Connolly's body is lean and muscular; his walk is graceful and fluid. Even strolling down to the shore break with his surfboard on his head, he looks like he's stalking prey.

"Hi!" she calls as he paddles toward her. "I got here early and I didn't think you were going to show. I mean, your past record hasn't been so good on that point." She giggles nervously, worried she might have offended him. "But you're here now, right? That's what matters. So, uh, what's this break called, huh? Do you come here often? Are you—"

He cuts her off with a wave of his hand. "Surf first, talk later."

"Okay, sure. Hey, did I tell you why I'm in Oahu? I mean, you must have been wondering, right? Have you ever seen that magazine *Water Woman*?"

He shoots her a bemused smile. "Are you going to surf or aren't you?"

"Surf? Oh, sure. Sure!" If he wants surfing, she'll show him surfing. In fact, she'll blow him away!

A wave is building up outside. Cricket paddles hard, suddenly more nervous than she ever felt at the ASA Western Championship. She drops in and cuts back hard, then pulls off a series of backside and frontside snaps that would make even the most jaded judge's jaw drop. She finishes with a sky-high off-the-lip.

She paddles back out, eager to see her father's reaction. She knows her dad isn't the effusive type, but she's hoping for a smile, or maybe even a few words of praise. But to her dismay, he's frowning as if she just dropped in on him.

"What was that?" he asks.

"What do you mean?"

"You looked like a blender on the grind setting. This is surfing, you know, not cooking."

"I *was* surfing," she said irritably. "I'm a shortboarder, not a longboarder like you. For us, it's all about shredding."

"Shortboard, longboard, it doesn't matter. Surfing is about reading the wave and reacting to it."

"That's what I was doing," she protests.

He shakes his head. "You were pulling off tricks just because you could. Okay, you were trying to impress me. Fine. But while you were throwing spray, you missed all the gifts the wave was trying to hand you."

"Gifts? Like what?"

"If you hadn't been rushing down the line, trying to pull off all those cutbacks, you could have pulled into the pocket and gotten some real speed. And while you were catching air, you threw away your chance for a floater that would have taken you to the inside section and another thirty seconds of ride time."

"Well, maybe," she concedes. "But that's not me. I can't lay back like that, just waiting for something to happen. I have to hit it hard. I have to charge it!"

Chet laughs. "I forgot. You're sixteen, with a lot to learn."

If he notices how tweaked Cricket is by his "lot to learn" jab, he doesn't let on. Instead, he takes off on a wave and shows her what he means. After a late take-off, he crouches in the shack for what seems like forever. Then, as the curl breaks over him, he soars up the face, pulls off a floater, and drops into the inside section. He walks to the nose and rides all the way to the beach.

"Okay, that was sweet," Cricket admits when he rejoins her in the lineup. "But I'm not going to be walking the nose on a six-foot-eight-inch tri-fin."

He shrugs. "I'm just saying, listen to the wave. It's like a conversation. It talks, you answer. What you say is up to you."

Have a conversation with the wave? Cricket rolls her eyes. Her dad is even loonier than she thought. *No wonder he couldn't live with Mom and me,* she tells herself. *We're way too normal.*

Still, the next wave she catches, she holds back a little. Not that she doesn't shred—shredding is as natural to Cricket as fidgeting—but she does pay a little more attention to what the wave is doing. She even floats over the whitewater to catch the inside section.

"Well?" she demands.

"Well, what?" he asks.

"Didn't you see me? I caught the inside section."

"I saw you."

That's it. No "Good job, Cricket." No "Why did I ever walk out on you, my beautiful, talented child?" Nope, none of that. He just takes off on the next wave and does his jungle cat/Zen master thing again. And, she has to admit, it's beautiful.

Weird, she thinks, *how he's so much like me and so different at the same time.*

When he was going off about the surf wax, he sounded just like her. He even tilted his head the same way she does. But now, out in the water, all that frenetic energy is focused in one direction, like sunlight focused through a magnifying glass. Chet "the Panther" Connolly is a surfing paradox—calm, cool, and on fire.

How does he do that? she wonders. She's determined to figure it out. Not that she wants to ride waves like her father does. She just wants to know she can.

So she takes off on the next one and tries again. This time she takes his advice to the extreme. Doesn't do any snaps, barely cuts back, just rides down the line. At first, it's practically painful to hold back like that. But after a while, she gets into it. It's like when she was first learning and it was all she could do to simply stay on the board and ride. Back then, that was enough.

Well, it isn't enough now, but it's not as boring as she imagined it would be. In fact, it's kind of fun to watch the wave unfold at her feet, feeling the energy surging forward, responding to its ebb and flow.

She paddles back out, certain that this time her father will be pleased. But before she can even make eye contact with him, he takes off on the next wave. Cricket stares after him, not sure whether to laugh or cry. Finally, she laughs and shakes her head. Her dad is so weird!

They spend the next hour surfing in silence. Not that Cricket wants it that way. She's dying to ask her father a million and one questions about the past. Even a simple, here-and-now question such as "What kind of surfboard are you riding?" would be nice. But every time she opens her mouth, he drops into another wave.

So she forces herself to turn her attention to her surfing, trying to follow her dad's advice to react to the waves instead of surfing them into submission. Sometimes it feels right and sometimes it doesn't. Half the time she can't stand holding back and she busts a big move just to prove she can.

But finally, she gets a ride that feels just right. She uses the wave's energy to fuel her moves, and for a moment, she does actually feel like she and the wave are having a conversation. When the wave finally collapses on the shore, she turns around, ready to paddle out again. But to her surprise, her father is paddling in.

"Nice ride," he says with just the hint of a smile.

Cricket feels giddy with joy. "Did you see that cutback?" she asks. "I dropped into the trough and picked up speed, then I flew up to the lip and—"

"I'll meet you here the day after tomorrow," he says. "Same time, okay?" He picks up his board and walks out of the water.

"Wait," she calls, splashing after him. "You said we could talk."

"I said surf first, talk later. We still have a lot of surfing to do."

"Hey, wait up. Dad!" It's a word she hasn't used much in the last ten years and it feels strange on her lips.

It must feel even stranger to Chet Connolly's ears because he doesn't respond. He just continues walking to the parking lot. Then he gets in his truck and drives away.

Cricket stands in the sand, watching him go. She

feels . . . well, she isn't sure exactly how she feels. Tired? Definitely. Happy? Excited? Yes, a little bit of both. Frustrated? For sure. And deep down, in a secret part of herself that she's kept locked up for a long, long time, she feels just a tiny bit hopeful.

9

Yum! That smells good!" Cricket exclaims, walking out to the lanai. It's the night of the luau, and Suzie Goldberg and her friends have arrived to set up the party.

Cricket watches as Suzie turns pieces of chicken on the backyard grill. "I love barbecued chicken," Cricket declares.

"In Hawaii, we call it 'huli huli chicken,'" Suzie replies. "*Huli* means 'turn it over,' and that's what we're going to do."

"Need some help?" Cate asks, walking out to join them. "We've got ten young hands and six old ones just raring to pitch in."

"You can carry out the casserole dishes we brought and spread them out on the patio table."

"Come on, Cricket," Cate says. "Let's round up the girls and get to work."

Soon all the girls are carrying food, plates, cups, and utensils out to the lanai. "What's this?" Rae asks, wrinkling her nose as she peeks into a serving dish.

One of Suzie's friends, a formidable Hawaiian man with a serious potbelly, takes a sniff and answers, "Squid luau. Good stuff!"

"Squid?" Luna gulps, stepping up beside her friend.

Rae nods. "In green goop."

"Pass," Luna says.

"That's what you think," her mother breaks in. "Suzie and her friends went to a lot of trouble to make this food. The least you can do is try it. Who knows? You might like it."

"Yeah, right, Mom," Luna mutters, rolling her eyes.

"First time I came to Hawaii," Josh says, passing them as they return to the kitchen, "someone offered me poi—steamed taro root pounded into a paste. There's one-finger, two-finger, and three-finger poi, depending on how thick it is. Well, I thought it looked pretty awful."

"And was it?" Rae asks.

"Well," Josh says, sighing loudly, "yes. But they say it's a little better if you mix it with fish or meat. Unfortunately I can't comment on that because I'm a vegetarian."

"Well, thanks, Josh," Cate says sarcastically. "That was exactly the message I was trying to get across to the girls."

Luna and Rae laugh while Josh fiddles with his glasses and hurries out to the lanai.

Soon everything is ready. The lanai has been decorated with strings of twinkling lights. Tiki torches burn in the sand. The table is covered with steaming casserole dishes and the coolers are filled with drinks. Huli huli chicken is browning on the grill. The only thing missing is the invited guests.

And then at last, the doorbell rings. Cricket runs to open the door—and freezes. It's Holly Beck and Keala Kennelly, two of the best female surfers in the world. "This is Suzie's party, right?" Holly asks.

"Yes," Cricket squeaks. "Come in."

And that's only the beginning. In the next hour, dozens more surfers show up. There are lots of Hawaiian locals, five or six white people like Suzie who grew up on Oahu, and a smattering of famous visitors— people like Taj Burrow, Rob Machado, and Kassia Meador.

The guests head for the food. To Cricket's amazement, almost everyone—even the Americans and the Australians—are trying everything. *Maybe I should, too,* she decides. "Come on," she tells her friends, "I need moral support. I'm going to hit the food table."

The girls gather around, piling their plates with chicken, poi, squid luau, and something called "ahi poke"—chunks of ahi tuna with seaweed. "You first," Luna tells Cricket.

"Yeah, it was your idea," Kanani agrees. "Go for it."

Cricket tackles the easy part first: the chicken. "Delicious!"

78

"That was no challenge," Isobel scoffs. "Try the rest."

Rae holds an imaginary microphone to her mouth. "Tonight on *Fear Factor,* a typical California teenager is forced to eat squid luau."

The girls giggle as Cricket lifts a forkful of squid to her lips. Closing her eyes, she takes a tiny, tentative bite. "Hey," she exclaims, as her eyes pop open, "this isn't half bad!"

Convinced, the girls dig in. Everyone except Isobel likes the squid. Only Kanani likes the poi. "It reminds me of the grits I ate in Florida," she explains. But all the girls like the ahi poki, and, of course, the huli huli chicken is an unequivocal hit.

Reggae, ska, and Jawaiian music—a local style of reggae with a laid-back, loping rhythm—are blasting through the speakers, and people are starting to dance in the sand. One of Suzie's friends—a beefy guy named Keake with wavy black hair and dimples—takes Cricket by the hand and leads her down the steps of the lanai. The local dance style is more laid-back than what Cricket is used to, and at first it's hard for her to slow down and get into the groove. But soon she's dancing like a local.

Everyone joins in, holding their drinks in their hands, singing along. Taj Burrow is dancing with Luna, and the other girls are dancing with good-looking local boys. Even Deirdre is dancing. Her partner is Suzie's friend, the guy with the serious potbelly!

It's a great scene, and Cricket knows she should relax and enjoy it. But where is Kainoa? He and his crew were invited—Suzie said so. So why isn't he here?

Keake leans in close, asking her what she thinks of Hawaii. He seems like a nice enough guy, but all Cricket can think about is Kainoa. She can't stop replaying their meeting at the waterfall. When he asked if she had come to steal his heart, she almost fainted. "Yes," she wants to tell him. "Yes, I did."

Just then, Cricket spots Kainoa walking up the beach with his friends Manu and Palani. She's dying to run out and meet him, but she controls herself. *No need to act too eager,* she tells herself. *He'll see me and come over.*

But if Kainoa sees her, he takes no notice. Instead, he and his friends walk around the dance floor and head for the lanai. After piling their plates with food, they stand in the corner, talking and eating together.

Cricket's heart sinks. What fun is dancing if it isn't with Kainoa? She tells Keake she's tired and leaves the dance floor. Then she hurries inside and flops down on her bed, too depressed to move.

She stays there until the music stops. *What's going on?* she wonders. *Is the party over already?*

Cricket gets up and walks to the door of her room. Suddenly, the soulful sound of a guitar fills the air. Then another instrument—higher and more percussive—joins in. Curious, Cricket walks out to the lanai. A group of local boys and girls are sitting on the steps, playing guitars and ukuleles. She steps closer, mesmerized. Then she sees that one of the ukulele players is Kainoa!

Now the boys and girls begin to sing, a beautiful song about a waterfall called "Akaka Falls." Next, they play a faster, good-time song called "Livin' on Easy." Everyone joins in on the chorus. Finally, they sing some songs in Hawaiian. Cricket can't understand the words, but she loves the way it sounds.

As the music ends and the crowd breaks up, Kainoa puts aside his ukulele and walks toward Cricket. "You want to go for a walk?" he asks.

Cricket's heart kicks into overdrive. "Okay."

Ska music is pounding through the speakers once again as they head off down the beach.

"Howzit, haole girl?" he asks.

"I'm fine. But I wish you'd quit calling me that. How would you like it if I called you 'brown boy'?"

He nods thoughtfully. "Fair enough. What you been up to since I saw you at the falls? You been surfing?"

"Yes, with my father." Cricket notices that Kainoa is slipping into pidgin as he talks with her. Could he be feeling more relaxed with her? she wonders.

"Your father's here with you?" Kai continues.

"Not exactly with me," she explains. "He's staying here for the season. Maybe you've heard of him. His name is Chet Connolly."

Kainoa looks at her with amazement. "Everybody's heard of him. He's been coming to the North Shore for years. And he's your father, eh? He's friends with

Ben Aipa, Greg Noll, all those guys, so I know he's gotta be a good man."

"He's a good surfer," Cricket declares, "but I don't know about the good man part. He walked out on my mother and me when I was little. The day before yesterday was the first time I'd seen him in ten years."

"Hey, that's not right. Why you think he left?"

"He won't tell me. He says, 'Surf first, talk later.'"

Kainoa thinks it over. "Some people don't show their feelings in words. They have other ways to communicate. Maybe with your father, it's surfing."

"I never thought of that."

"Same goes for my father. He didn't say much. He'd rather fish, surf, play music. But when we did those things together, we didn't need words."

"Why are you talking past tense?" Cricket asks. "Did your father leave, too?"

"You could say that. He died when I was thirteen."

"Oh, Kainoa, I'm sorry!"

"Yeah, I miss him every day. But your father's still around. Maybe he hasn't always been there for you, but now you've got a second chance. You're lucky, Cricket."

Lucky? She never thought of it that way. But maybe Kainoa is right.

"Kainoa," she says, "can I ask you something? When you first showed up at the party, why didn't you come over and say hello to me?"

He shrugs. "I was with my bruddahs. We had to

check out the scene, say hello to the people we know. If I went off with you first thing, the bruddahs would feel insulted."

"But it's okay now?"

He grins. "I don't care. I couldn't wait any longer. I want to be with you."

Cricket's heart starts to flutter. "I want to be with you, too."

"Look," Kainoa says, pointing to the almost-full moon hanging over the water. He slips his arm around her waist and pulls her close.

Cricket is so nervous and excited, she can barely stand still. "It's so beautiful here," she babbles. "The ocean, the mountains, the birds, the flowers. It's paradise!"

"When I'm with you, it feels that way," he whispers. He plucks a red hibiscus flower from a nearby bush. Brushing aside her hair, he gently places it behind her ear.

"And—and the food," she yammers. "I didn't think I'd like it, but I do. Even the squid and the ahi and stuff. It's—"

Kainoa cuts her off with a kiss. Her head is spinning as he pulls her close. She's never met anyone like Kainoa before. His smooth, brown skin and black, wavy hair make her feel weak inside. But his wise comments about her father make her feel strong. It's a sweet combination, and one she wants to keep on experiencing.

Paradise? Cricket puts her head on Kainoa's shoulder and smiles. She's found it—right here, right now.

10

Cricket is having a beautiful dream. She's surfing with Kainoa, the two of them taking turns shredding on the biggest, most picture-perfect waves imaginable. On the shore, her dad is watching and nodding approvingly. Then Cricket and Kainoa paddle in and sit side by side in the warm sand.

"Don't leave, Cricket," Kainoa whispers. "Promise me you'll stay on the North Shore and surf with me forever."

Suddenly, a loud, percussive sound breaks the stillness. Reluctantly, Cricket's eyes flutter open. Kainoa disappears, along with the warm sand and the epic waves. Now she's lying in her bed in the gray morning light while Deirdre claps her hands and proclaims, "Everybody up! We're leaving for Lili'u's Reef in exactly ten minutes!"

In the next bed, Kanani rubs her eyes. "What?" she

asks in a drowsy voice. "You mean the locals said it was okay?"

"Seems our little luau did the trick," Deirdre proclaims happily. "Suzie and I had a talk with some of them last night and they've agreed to let us photograph anywhere we want. No hassles, no dropping in. In return, we won't print the names of any actual surf spots or reveal their locations."

Cricket yawns and sits up. "But I thought that was why you wanted to shoot at Oahu's secret spots—so *Water Woman*'s readers could be the first to know about them."

"That would have been sweet, I admit," Deirdre agrees. "But hey, you take what you can get. At least our fashion spread will have lots of local color. And who knows? Maybe we can drop a few hints about the spots—just enough to get our readers salivating while still keeping the people happy."

Cricket wonders if that's possible. But she's got more pressing concerns on her mind at the moment. Will Kainoa be in the water today? Will he pay attention to her? Or possibly—and this would be beyond her wildest dreams—even treat her like his girlfriend?

Eagerly, Cricket hops out of bed and slips into the eye-catching floral-print bikini that Deirdre has left for her. She walks into the bathroom and checks herself out. *Not bad,* she thinks. Her hair suddenly appears fuller, her body more shapely. Even her freckles seem okay to her today.

"Am I getting prettier?" she asks the girl in the mirror. Or maybe it's something else. She's heard that love can give you a special glow. Is that what she's seeing?

Well, she tells herself, *whatever it is, I like it.* Then she adds in a whisper, "And I hope Kainoa does, too."

Fifteen minutes later, the girls are standing at Lili'u's Reef. It's a perfect day—four- to six-foot waves, no wind, not a cloud in the sky. Cricket stands on tiptoe, searching for Kainoa in the lineup. There are five or six guys out, but none of them have Kainoa's long hair.

Josh is checking the water housing on his camera. He pulls on his flippers, grabs his boogie board, and gazes nervously at the surf.

"Maybe you should learn to swim," Isobel suggests.

"Where's the fun in that?" Rae snickers.

Josh nods seriously. "When my adrenaline is pumping, I take better photos." He slogs into the shore break, camera in hand. "Now come on, girls. Let's go surfing!"

With Cate by their side, the girls paddle out. When they reach the lineup, Cricket sits up and glances at the guys. Manu and Palani are there, plus a couple of other boys she recognizes from the luau. She catches Manu's eye and smiles. To her delight, he nods, a faint smile on his lips.

At Cate's urging, the girls hold back for a while, allowing the local boys to catch the best and biggest waves. Cricket sits on her board, restlessly cracking her knuckles. Oh, how she longs to take off on one of those beautiful grinders!

For the tenth time in less than a minute, she gazes toward the shore, looking for Kainoa. Just then, a surfboard breaks through the back of a collapsing wave. It's Kainoa, his long hair flowing behind him as he paddles toward her.

"Kainoa! Over here!" she calls, totally unable to keep her cool.

This time, to her great relief, he doesn't ignore her. "What you doing sitting out here like a frog on a lily pad?" he asks with a grin.

"Cate said to hold back and leave the big waves for you and your crew."

"There's plenty waves for everybody," he replies. He glances at Manu and Palani. "Right, bruddahs?"

"Today we share," Palani agrees.

"Geevum!" Manu calls.

"That means 'go for it,'" Kainoa explains.

Cricket doesn't hesitate. When the next set rolls through, she takes off. Her first instinct is to shred hard, really show the boys what she can do. But then she remembers her father's words. *"Listen to the wave. It's like a conversation. It talks, you answer."*

Okay, that's easy, she thinks. *This wave is shouting, "Major barrel!"*

Her answer is to hold back, and then sail into the

green room. She reaches out and touches the water, reading the wave face like a page of Braille. She holds on, adjusts her position, then *whoosh!* The tube spits her out into the sunlight. As she throws herself into a final backside snap, she notices Josh floating nearby on his boogie board, taking her photograph.

"Beauty!" he shouts, giving her the thumbs-up sign.

Cricket waves and paddles back out. She feels energized, like she just gulped down a whole bag of M&M's.

"I've never seen you surf quite like that, Cricket," Cate says as she rejoins the lineup.

Coming from a former pro like Cate Martin, that's quite a compliment. Cricket grins, but right now there's one opinion that's even more important to her. She looks at Kainoa, who's just paddling out after his own ride.

"Shaka, girl!" he says, cruising up beside her. "I didn't know you could surf so good."

Cricket feels like leaping off her board and hugging him. Instead, she puts her hands on her hips and says, "That's because last time you didn't give me a chance."

Kainoa looks deep into her eyes. "You ask politelike, Cricket, I give you all the chances you want."

Cricket meets his gaze and suddenly she feels like she's leaping off the rocks at Kapena Falls. "Okay," she breathes.

"Hey, 'nuff talk, brah," Manu calls. "Less'go!"

Kainoa looks over his shoulder. A pretty little wave

is rolling in. "You heard what the bruddah said," he calls to Cricket. "Less'go!"

They take off together and ride the wave side by side. "Hey, haole girl," Kainoa calls teasingly, "get offa my wave!"

"Make me!" Cricket calls back.

Kainoa shoots her a menacing look. "You know what we call this look? Stink eye! Pretty scary, huh?"

"Not hardly, dude! You don't scare me!"

"Oh, yeah?" He laughs and reaches out to shove her. She shoves back and, with a scream, they both fall backward off their boards.

As Cricket swims to the surface, she feels Kainoa's hand reach for hers. He pulls her close and kisses her underwater. Then, laughing and gasping for air, they both pop up into the warm Hawaiian sunshine.

Three hours later, happy and exhausted, the California girls and the Hawaiian boys paddle in together. Deirdre is waiting for them, a beaming smile on her face.

"Fantastic!" she tells the girls. "All five of you looked gorgeous, just gorgeous! This is going to be our best swimwear preview ever!"

For the boys, she has only a closed-mouth smile. "Thank you, gentlemen. I appreciate your hospitality."

Josh staggers in a moment later, sand in his hair and a weary look on his face. "Nice work, girls," he pants, collapsing in the sand. "Will someone please get me a water?"

Deirdre tosses him a bottle and turns back to the girls. "Let's go, gang. We have two hours for lunch and a shower. Then we're heading to the Foster Botanical Garden for our next photo session."

"This afternoon?" Cricket cries.

"You have a problem with that?"

"When do we get some time off?" Kanani asks.

That's what Cricket is wondering, too. As far as she's concerned, modeling is getting old. She'd rather spend the afternoon with Kainoa.

"Sorry, girls, but this isn't a vacation," Deirdre says. "It's a modeling shoot. *Water Woman* expects me to come home with some hot photos and a can't-put-it-down article, and that's what I plan to do."

The girls let out a collective groan, but Deirdre ignores them and starts marching up the beach like a drill sergeant leading a bunch of raw recruits.

With a sigh, Cricket turns to Kainoa. "See you later, I guess."

"Hey," he says, "you gotta eat, right? You ever try Spam moosabi?"

"Spam *what*?"

He laughs. "Come on. I'm gonna take you to my house for lunch."

Cricket runs to Cate and tells her about Kainoa's invitation. "Please?" she begs. "I'll be back before we leave for the garden, I promise."

Cate smiles. "I had a Hawaiian boyfriend once, too. That was a long time ago, before I met Luna's dad." She pauses, apparently thinking it over. "Go on," she says at last. "I'll take your surfboard. But if you're not back by one o'clock, I'll have your head on a platter."

Cricket gives Cate a heartfelt hug. No doubt about it. She *is* the coolest mother who ever lived!

With her heart soaring, Cricket runs back to Kainoa. "Let's go."

"You ready for a hike?"

"Where do you live?" she asks anxiously. Maybe this is going to take longer than she realized.

He points about a quarter mile down the beach to a red corrugated-tin roof poking up between the palm trees. "There."

Cricket lets out a sigh of relief. "Lead on."

Waving good-bye to their friends, they walk into a neighborhood of small, wooden houses. Kainoa's house is on the corner, facing the ocean. On the lanai, a rope hammock swings invitingly in the breeze.

A little girl, maybe seven or eight years old, appears from behind a mango tree. "Who's that?" she asks, eyeing Cricket suspiciously.

"My friend Cricket. Cricket, this is my sister, Moana."

"You don't look like a cricket," Moana says.

"But I hop like one," Cricket replies, bouncing toward the little girl, who shrieks with delight and runs back behind the tree.

Kainoa leans his surfboard against the house. "My mom's at work," he says. "Come on in."

"Where does she work?" Cricket asks as she follows him into the small, cozy living room. The mouthwatering smell of steamed rice and fried meat fills the air.

"She owns Puka's Plate Lunch in Haleiwa."

"I ate there!" Cricket exclaims. "It's good."

"My grandparents opened the place back in the sixties. When they retired, my dad took it over. Since he died, Mom's been running it by herself."

"That must be a lot of work," Cricket remarks, stepping over the blocks and dolls that are scattered across the floor.

He nods. "She's gone a lot. When I graduate in June, I'll go to work there full-time."

"I bet she's looking forward to that."

He shrugs and looks away. "My dad wanted my sister and me to go to college. But I guess that's not going to happen now."

Cricket is about to reply when an elderly woman in a flowered dress walks into the room. Her nut-brown face is crisscrossed with wrinkles and her gray hair is pulled back into a bun.

"Grams," Kainoa says, "this is my friend Cricket."

"Aloha. Are you one of the girls from the surfing magazine?"

Cricket nods, pleased to learn that Kainoa has been talking about her. "We just finished our photo session at Lili'u's Reef."

"Then you must be hungry."

"I told her you were making Spam moosabi," Kainoa says. "She wants to try it."

"Yes, but first I want to know what it is," Cricket answers warily.

Grams laughs. "Look, I show you." She reaches in a drawer and takes out a rectangular plastic mold, about one inch wide and two inches long. Lifting a slice of fried Spam from the frying pan, she lays it in the mold. Then she adds rice, and tops it with another piece of Spam. Finally, she presses the block of Spam and rice out of the mold and wraps a strip of dried seaweed around it.

"Try it," Kainoa says encouragingly.

Cricket hesitates. The stuff looks totally weird, but what's she going to do? She can't be rude. Finally, she picks up the Spam moosabi and takes a tentative bite. The salty Spam and starchy rice are delicious! Even the seaweed isn't too bad. "Hey, it's good!" she exclaims.

Grams nods approvingly. "You *keiki* go sit on the lanai. I bring you more moosabi and some mango juice."

Cricket and Kainoa walk outside and sit at the picnic table. Warm sunlight filters through the palm trees. Down the street, children are laughing. Cricket lets out a satisfied sigh. *Is this what Hawaiians mean when they say "hang loose"?* she wonders. If so, she likes it.

Kainoa reaches across the table and takes her hand.

"You looked good out there this morning. And I don't just mean your surfing. In that bikini, you chicken skin *kine nani*."

"What?"

"You're so pretty you give me goose bumps."

Cricket giggles, but inside she's melting like shave ice on a hot day. She wonders how you say *hottie* in Hawaiian, but just then Grams walks out with the food. Cricket and Kainoa jump apart. Grams looks out toward the ocean and shouts, "Moana! Get out of that water! Now!"

Cricket turns to see Kainoa's sister running back from the water's edge. "What's wrong?" Cricket asks.

"There's an underwater pipe out there that pumps treated sewage into the ocean," Kainoa explains. "It's pretty close to the shore, and since they built the new resort upstream, the output is so high it's dangerous."

Cricket frowns. "You'd better call the water department and tell them about that."

Grams snorts a laugh. "You think nobody has tried? A little pollution in this neighborhood isn't going to get much attention. This isn't Waikiki, you know."

Grams goes back into the house, and Kainoa and Cricket turn to their food. It's delicious, and being with Kainoa is Cricket's idea of heaven. Still, she can't quite recapture that "hang loose" feeling she had just a few moments ago. She keeps thinking about the pipe that's pumping sewage into the ocean.

But what can I do about it? she wonders.

She's just a visitor to the island, and although she hates to think about it, she knows she'll be going home soon. While she's here, she doesn't want anything to spoil her perfect moment in paradise. So she pushes all the bad thoughts out of her head, and just concentrates on Kainoa's handsome face.

11

*T*he next morning, Cricket is up before dawn. Once again, she slips out of the house undetected and jogs down the empty beach to meet her father. This time he's in the water when she arrives, and she understands why. Head-high surf is blasting off the craggy, offshore rock, forming fast, powerful bowls.

Cricket waves to her father and starts paddling out. But she's only three-quarters of the way to the lineup when a big set rolls in. On impulse, she turns around and takes off on a huge breaker. It's a late takeoff that sends her flying up the ledge. Paddling for all she's worth, she free-falls down the face—and manages to hang on! She touches down and sails into a barrel, only to have it close out on her a second later.

She comes up panting but exhilarated. She can't wait to see what her father has to say about her amazing recovery! She paddles through the exploding whitewater until she catches sight of him. "Hi!" she calls.

"What the hell was that?" he asks grimly.

"What do you mean?"

"That stupid late takeoff. You could have broken your neck on the coral."

"Yeah, but I didn't. And did you see the way I recovered and made the wave?"

"Use your brain, Cricket. If you'd finished your paddle and waited until you were in position, you would have had a real ride."

Cricket looks away, trying not to care what her father thinks. "Too bad there wasn't a photographer around," she mutters. "I probably would have made the cover of *Surfing*."

"Is that all you care about? Getting your photo on the cover of a magazine? Then why don't you go surf the Waimea shore break? You'll probably end up a paraplegic, but what's a little thing like that compared to fifteen minutes of fame?"

"I'd be doing better than you," she says defiantly. "You could have been one of the best surfers in the world, but you stopped competing. Now you're just some weirdo has-been from the sixties!"

Dad looks stunned, like someone just punched him in the stomach, and Cricket instantly regrets her words. She's waited so long to get her father back in her life. Now, with one foolish outburst, she's probably driven him away for another ten years.

Then, to her amazement, her father starts to laugh. "It's scary how much you remind me of myself at sixteen. You're a big ball of nervous energy without a lick of sense."

"Look, I didn't mean what I said," she tells him. "I don't even know what I'm talking about. It's just something I heard Mom say—how you competed in a few Malibu contests and then dropped out of the whole surfing scene."

Dad just shakes his head and continues laughing.

"Hey," she grumbles, regret turning to irritation, "stop laughing at me."

"I'm not laughing at you," he says, still chuckling. "I'm laughing at *me*. Well, the me I used to be. But I suppose my current self is just as ridiculous—a screwed-up middle-aged man trying to reconnect with his teenage daughter by giving her surf tips."

Cricket can't help but smile. "It does kind of sound like a Movie of the Week."

Dad shrugs. "Look, all I'm saying is slow down a little. Remember what I said about having a conversation with the wave? That last ride was more like a boxing match."

But Cricket isn't listening. Now that she knows her father isn't offended, she wants to find out the truth. "Why did you stop competing after just a few contests?" she asks.

"Enough talk." He motions toward the horizon where a new set is forming. "Let's surf."

"But Dad—"

Ignoring her, he paddles into position and takes off on a wave. Seconds later, he disappears into a spitting bowl and snags one of the longest tube rides Cricket has ever seen.

Cricket sighs and shakes her head. There are so many things she wants to tell her father, and so many questions she wants to ask him. But who knows if he'll ever be ready to talk to her?

Well, she thinks, *while I'm waiting to find out, I might as well follow Dad's lead and catch a wave.*

She can hear his voice in her head as she takes off. *Slow down. Read the wave and react to it.* She drops in and resists the urge to throw some spray. Instead, she looks ahead and sees a perfect barrel forming. Charging into it, she's suddenly surrounded by water, getting the longest, most perfect tube ride of her entire life.

"See you here tomorrow morning," Dad says as they wade out of the shore break.

By now, Cricket knows better than to ask for more. "Okay," she replies.

To her surprise, her father tosses his board in the sand and sits down. Motioning for Cricket to sit beside him, he gazes out at the waves and says, "Your mother's right. I probably could have been famous if I'd known how to play the game."

"What do you mean?" Cricket asks.

"Back in the sixties, when I started surfing, it wasn't like it is today. There were no magazines, no contests, no sponsors. We were just a bunch of guys hanging out at the beach, catching some waves. Then the *Gidget* movie came out and the Beach Boys started singing about surfing safaris. Suddenly, the whole scene just exploded."

Cricket nods, worried that anything more might distract her father from his story.

"Some of the guys knew how to take advantage of what was happening," he continues, still looking out to sea. "They won contests, got their photos in magazines, put out their own signature surfboards, all that. But me—I couldn't handle it. I'd always been shy, kind of a loner. I didn't feel comfortable giving interviews or posing for pictures. And the whole contest scene just turned me off. I wasn't surfing to win trophies. For me, it was all about soul."

"But you surfed in a couple of contests," Cricket says, unable to hold back. "I've seen the photos."

"First place in both. I guess I just wanted to prove I could do it. But after that I dropped out of the whole scene. I didn't stop surfing, but I stayed away from the popular spots. If anybody recognized me or tried to take my photo, I got out of the water and left." He smiles. "Funny thing is it just seemed to make my reputation grow. People called me 'the Panther' and made up all these crazy stories about me—said I'd surfed fifty-foot Keana Point, rubbish like that." He shakes his head at the absurdity of it all. "I was becoming a legend, but all I wanted was for people to leave me alone and let me surf."

"This was before I was born?" Cricket asks.

He nods. "Then I fell in love with Chelsea—your mom—and everything changed. I knew she wasn't going to be interested in a part-time handyman living in a run-down shack on Pacific Coast Highway. So I went to work for Dooley Surfboards—designed a signature surfboard for them, even lent my name to a line of surf trunks. It worked for a while, but I hated the whole corporate scene, and Danny Dooley and I were constantly clashing over one thing or another. I wanted to quit, but then Chelsea got pregnant with you."

"Was that a problem?" Cricket asks, even though she's pretty sure she knows the answer.

"No," he says quickly. Then he sighs. "Well, yes. I mean, *you* weren't the problem. It was me. Your mom was pressuring me to stay with Dooley, make more money, move up in the company."

"But didn't she see how you hated it?"

He shrugs. "She wanted to give you a good life. She had good intentions, but she was talking to the wrong guy. The longer I stayed with Dooley, the more miserable I became. I was fighting at work, fighting at home. Finally, I got fired and Chelsea really laid into me. I felt like a total failure. So I left. I figured the less you saw of me, the better. I knew your mother would take better care of you than I ever could." He hesitates. "She has, hasn't she?"

Cricket hugs her knees. "She's done okay, I guess. But she works too much. I mean, she's practically never home. And she doesn't like it that I surf. She doesn't come right out and say it, but I can feel it. I guess it reminds her of you."

He laughs humorlessly. "No doubt."

"Dad," Cricket burst out, "I'm nothing like Mom. I don't look like her, or talk like her, and I sure don't think like her. Sometimes I feel like I'm living with a stranger."

"Don't say that," Dad says sternly. "You don't want to be like me. Your mother is practical and sensible, and she's sweet and funny, too—or at least she used to be."

"But I'm a surfer like you. It's all I care about."

For the first time since they started talking, Dad turns to look at her. "Cricket, I tried to stay out of your life, but when I heard you were surfing seriously, I just had to see for myself. I came to watch you at the Western Championship last summer. Did you know that?"

Cricket frowns, remembering the devastating disappointment she felt when her father didn't show up to cheer her on. But now he says he *was* there. If only he had shown himself! It would have made such a difference. "Where were you?" she asks. "Why didn't you talk to me?"

"I was up on the bluffs. I . . . I didn't know what to say to you. I don't know now. But here you are, getting

102

in my face and asking all sorts of difficult questions. What am I supposed to do?"

"Surf?" she asks with a wry smile.

But Dad doesn't smile back. "Do you hate me, Cricket?" he asks.

She gazes at her dad. Right now, he looks as worried and vulnerable as a toddler. She thinks about his question. She doesn't totally understand him, and she's not quite ready to forgive him—not yet. But . . .

"No," she says honestly. "I don't hate you."

He looks her straight in the eye—the first time ever. "Thank you." Then he jumps to his feet and grabs his board.

"Wait!" she calls as he strides toward his truck. "I have more questions I want to ask you."

But it's obvious he isn't ready to answer them. Without a backward glance, he starts his truck and drives away.

Cricket hurries through the back door, tripping on the step in her excitement. She hears Deirdre's sleepy voice calling, "Who's there?" Quickly, she tiptoes into her bedroom, eager to tell Kanani what just happened.

"Kanani," she whispers, shaking the curled-up figure in the bed. "Wake up! You remember how stoked I was yesterday when Kainoa asked me over for lunch? Well, as if that wasn't enough, listen to this—my father talked to me! I mean, really talked. He told me why he dropped out of the surf scene, and why he walked out on my mom and me, and . . . everything. And Kanani, you'll never believe this. He was at the Western Championship. He—"

Cricket freezes as a strangled sob explodes from Kanani's lips. Pulling back, she stares down at her friend. "Kanani, what is it? What's wrong?"

"I . . . I'm happy for you, Cricket," she chokes. "Honestly, I am. It's just . . . oh, Cricket, why can't things work out for me the way they're working out for you? I can't even bring myself to talk to my birthfather. And even if I did, so what? He's not going to have a big heart-to-heart with me like your dad just did with you."

"You don't know that," Cricket protests.

"Yes I do. It's different for us. He didn't want me then, and he won't want me now. And then there's Francisco."

Francisco is Kanani's boyfriend. He lives in Florida, near Sebastian Inlet. They met in August when she traveled there for a longboard contest. "What about him?" Cricket asks.

"Forget it. I sound like such a crybaby."

"No you don't. Come on, tell me."

"I haven't been able to e-mail him since we got to Hawaii. Oh, Cricket, I miss him so much. And who knows if I'll even see him again? Florida and California are so far away."

Cricket feels terrible that her happiness has made her friend so sad. Hugging her, she says, "You poor thing. Look, Deirdre said we have the morning free, right? Let's go into Haleiwa and find an Internet café. I bet you have about a dozen e-mails waiting for you from Francisco."

"You think so?" she sniffles.

"Totally. Once you read them and write back, you'll feel much better. And then we'll drive into Honolulu, find the office of the *Oahu Daily News,* and meet your father."

Kanani stiffens. "No way!"

Cricket laughs. "Okay, okay. Just kidding." She reaches under her pillow and pulls out a bag of Skittles. "Want some?"

"You take those to bed with you?" Kanani asks in astonishment.

Cricket shrugs. "Never know when I'm going to need a little midnight sugar boost."

Kanani giggles. "Cricket, you are insane!"

Cricket grabs a pillow and holds it menacingly over Kanani's head. "Those are fighting words, girlfriend."

Kanani is on her feet in an instant. "Pillow fight!" she screams. Within seconds, Luna, Rae, and Isobel appear, pillows in hand.

Cricket laughs. She loves her friends. She throws out her arms and cries, "You guys are so—" But she doesn't get any further because at that moment, a barrage of pillows smack her right in the face.

12

*I*t's the morning after Cricket's big talk with her father. She rolls over in bed and hugs her pillow, dreaming that it's Kainoa.

"Aaaahhh!"

Cricket's eyes pop open. Did someone scream, or was it just a dream? "Kanani, did you hear that?"

Kanani is sitting bolt upright in the next bed, blinking at the early morning sunlight. "Uh-huh."

"It sounded a little like Deirdre," Cricket says. "Maybe Josh finally got fed up with her bossy ways and strangled her."

Kanani snickers. A second later, Deirdre's voice reverberates through the house. "Everyone in the living room! *Now!*"

"Darn, she's still alive," Cricket mutters, slipping into a T-shirt and a pair of shorts.

She and Kanani hurry into the living room. Cate,

Luna, Rae, and Isobel appear a moment later. Josh is standing there with his arsenal of cameras. The back of each camera is open and there's no film in any of them. Deirdre stands beside him, looking like she just witnessed a bank robbery.

"What do you know about this?" she demands, pointing at Josh's cameras.

"They work better with film in them, I can tell you that," Cricket quips.

"Don't be smart!" Deirdre cries. "Does anyone have any idea who stole our film?"

"What are you talking about?" Luna's mom asks.

"I woke up a few minutes ago and heard a sound in the living room," Josh explains. "When I went to see what it was, I found my cameras open and all the film gone."

"You mean, the film you shot of us?" Luna asks in disbelief.

Josh nods. "If it was only the film in the cameras that was missing, it wouldn't be so bad. Those rolls were only partly exposed. But the thief took everything—the rolls we shot at Lili'u's Reef, at the shave ice shack, the waterfall, the botanical garden. Everything."

Cricket feels totally confused. "Why would somebody do that?" she asks.

"This is a disaster!" Deirdre fumes, ignoring her question. "The deadline for the spring swimwear issue is coming up in just three days. Josh was going to send the film back to California by FedEx tomorrow."

"Can't we reshoot the photos?" Luna's mom asks.

Deirdre frowns, thinking it over. "Frankly, I don't know if we have time to reshoot at all these locations. I'll have to call my editor. But first, I'm calling the police."

The girls wait anxiously as Deirdre calls 911 and explains what happened. "These aren't tourist photos," she barks into the phone. "This was a fashion shoot for a surfing magazine. We're talking big bucks here!"

Finally, she slams down the phone and says, "The police are on their way. Don't touch anything. They might want to dust for fingerprints."

Next, she calls her editor. Cricket and her friends exchange worried expressions as they hear Deirdre say, "You could handle that in California? Are you sure? Well, when would you want us back?"

"What's going on?" Rae asks as Deirdre hangs up the phone. "What did they say?"

Cricket has never seen Deirdre when she wasn't marching around like a major general. But now her shoulders are slumped and her feet are dragging. "If we can't get the film back, they're going to scale down the swimwear preview and reshoot it in California with a group of professional models."

"But that's boring!" Cricket cries. "The whole point was to use real surfer girls."

"In real surf," Kanani adds.

"Local color," Luna says.

"Secret spots," Isobel declares.

"I know all that," Deirdre snaps. "I thought up the

concept, remember? But what can I do? My hands are tied."

Cricket can't believe her ears! After all the hard work they've put in, she can't stand the thought of a bunch of professional models posing for the swimsuit preview. Besides, what will she tell the kids at school? Her neighbors? Her relatives? They're all expecting to see her photo in *Water Woman* magazine.

"What a letdown!" Rae groans, putting everybody's thoughts into words.

Luna's mom stands up. "Come on, girls. Let's go surfing."

"Surfing?" Cricket cries. "Now?"

"Why not? Look, sitting around moping isn't going to do any good. Until we hear what the police have to say, we might as well get in some water time."

Everyone turns to Deirdre for her approval. "Go ahead," she says, shooing them away. "You're just going to be in the way around here. If the cops need to question you, I'll send them down to the beach."

"Lili'u's Reef," Luna's mom exclaims, "here we come!"

Cricket paddles her board through the warm, blue water, happy to be doing something with her body besides fidgeting. Back at the house, she felt so confused, so helpless. Now, with the sun on her shoulders and the wild waves crashing all around her, she can almost imagine everything is going to be all right. The cops will catch the thief and recover the photos. The magazine will come out and the girls will be the toast of the surfing community.

"And Kainoa and I will be in love forever," Cricket whispers.

She laughs. Where did *that* crazy thought come from? She barely knows Kainoa. How can she imagine she's in love with him, or vice versa?

And yet, why not? Everything about him thrills her—his handsome face, his powerful surfing, his knowledge of Hawaiian culture. She wants to be around him every minute of every day. If that isn't love, she wonders, what is?

And he cares for her, too, doesn't he? She remembers the happy grin on his face when they were surfing together, and the loving look in his eyes when he told her "you chicken skin kine nani." You're so pretty you give me goose bumps. No one has ever said anything like that to her before. And then, when he kissed her—wow!

Cricket paddles into the lineup just in time to see an enormous sea turtle surface, take a breath, and disappear beneath the waves. She stares, stunned and delighted, and then looks around for someone to share her excitement with. The first person she sees is Kainoa's friend Manu.

"Did you see the turtle?" she calls.

To her surprise, he turns away. Cricket frowns, bewildered. *Maybe he didn't hear me,* she thinks, turning her attention to the surf. A wave is coming and she's in position. Eagerly, she paddles into it. But just as she drops in, Manu takes off in front of her.

"Hey!" she shouts, but he ignores her and continues surfing, carving every inch of open wave face and driving her back into the whitewater.

Baffled and frustrated, Cricket pulls out and looks around to see how the other girls are faring. To her dismay, she soon realizes her girlfriends are having the same experience. The locals are cutting them off, ignoring them, or worse yet, dissing them.

Then Cricket spots Kainoa paddling out. Quickly, she paddles over to meet him. "I'm so glad you're here," she calls. "Your friends are acting totally weird—snaking our waves and stuff, just like the first time we tried to surf here. I can't figure out what's going on."

"You can't, huh?" he replies. "Well, maybe they don't like being double-crossed. You ever think of that?"

"Double-crossed? What are you talking about?"

"Go ask your father, yeah? He's the one who found out what Deirdre's planning to do."

"Deirdre? Planning to do what?"

"Don't play dumb, haole girl. We local boys aren't as lolo as you think. You take our aloha and spit on it, we're not gonna take it lying down."

"Kainoa, please, I don't understand what you're talking about," she cries. "Honest I don't."

"Okay, you want me to spell it out? Deirdre promised she wouldn't reveal the names or locations of our secret spots, yeah? Only she lied. She's gonna tell everything in her article. She's even gonna include maps."

Cricket is so stunned, she can't speak. Finally, she sputters, "How do you know?"

"I told you. Your father found out."

"But how would he get that kind of information?"

"I don't know the details. But everyone on the North Shore knows the Panther doesn't lie. Besides, I talked it over with my father. He tells me, 'Don't trust that lady. She's bad news for the kamaaina.'"

"But I—I thought your father was dead," Cricket stammers.

"He is, but when I see the turtles swimming here at the reef, I feel him with me. His spirit is alive in the ocean."

With that, Kainoa paddles away, leaving Cricket feeling so confused she can't even think straight. Is what Kainoa said about Deirdre true? If it is, how did her father find out? And does his discovery have something to do with the theft of the photos?

Then suddenly, Cricket remembers the sea turtle she saw diving into the waves as she paddled out. Is it true? Could Kainoa's father's spirit be present? And trying to tell her something?

Get real, Cricket, she tells herself. *That's just plain crazy.*

Or is it? Cricket isn't sure of anything anymore. All she knows is she has to talk to her father. But first, she has to find him.

Cricket drives the red Xterra down the narrow driveway beside Sunset Sensations. At the end of the driveway, she sees a small ramshackle wooden house. According to the guys at the Haleiwa Surf Shop, this is where her father is staying.

Chomping on her gum to calm her nerves, she parks the car and walks up to the house. She's about to knock when her father appears at the screen door. "Where were you this morning?" he asks.

"What do you mean?" And then it hits her. She was supposed to go surfing with her father! "Oh, man, I forgot. Everything's been so crazy. Someone stole all the film that Josh took of us. Then we went surfing at Lili'u's Reef and the crowd there totally dissed us. Then Kainoa said you found out Deirdre's planning to reveal the location of their secret surf spots in her article. Dad, what's going on?"

He steps outside and lets the screen door slam behind him. "I don't know anything about the photos. But I do know that Deirdre is a complete ass."

"Huh? You don't even know her, do you?"

"No, and I don't want to, either."

"Dad, what are you talking about?"

"I was in the Paradise Club last night, listening to some music. There was a lady at the next table mouthing off to her friends about how she scored a big coup for *Water Woman* magazine. According to her, she convinced the local surfers to let the magazine shoot a swimwear spread at Lili'u's Reef and a few other local spots. The deal was the article wouldn't identify the spots, but she figured all bets were off once she left the island. Not only does she plan to name the spots, she plans to tell her readers how to get to them."

"Are you sure it was Deirdre?" Cricket asks.

"That's what her friends called her," Dad says. "Besides, you know anyone else writing a swimwear preview for *Water Woman*?"

"Okay, okay. But why couldn't you just have talked to Deirdre directly? Why did you have to tell Kainoa and his friends to steal the film?"

Dad looks puzzled. "Who's this Kainoa you keep talking about? All I did was tell my buddy Eddie Hamura what I heard. Maybe he told some other local guys and they took things into their own hands. I don't know." He shrugs. "That part is none of my business."

"None of your business?" Cricket cries. "Thanks to you, *Water Woman* is reshooting the swimwear preview in California. My friends and I aren't even going to be in it. How do you think that makes me feel?"

Dad gazes at her with a furrowed brow. "I'm sorry if I did something to hurt you, Cricket. I didn't mean to. But to be honest, I don't understand why you'd want to be in a magazine that has so little respect for the kamaaina."

Cricket feels so exasperated, she wants to scream. She came to Oahu filled with such high expectations. She couldn't wait to meet the people, see the sights, and surf the waves of the North Shore. But instead of welcoming her, everyone she's met—from Suzie to Kainoa to her father—has lectured her. Respect the locals. Don't reveal their secret spots. Slow down. Listen to the wave. And she's tried—really she has. But no matter what she does, it never seems to be enough.

"I'm tired of the kama-whatever and their stupid problems," she cries. "What about *my* problems?" When her father doesn't answer, she rolls her eyes. "Oh, excuse me, I forgot. My problems don't interest you. You made that clear ten years ago when you walked out on Mom and me."

"Cricket, please," Dad says. "This has nothing to do with you. I was just trying to keep that Deirdre woman from cheating my friends."

"Nothing to do with me? All I ever wanted was to make it as a surfer. When *Water Woman* chose the girls and me to be in their big swimwear issue, I couldn't believe it. Everyone in the international surf scene was going to see my photo and read about me. It was a dream come true. And now you've screwed it up!"

Dad winces. "Cricket, I didn't know that kind of exposure was so important to you. I never cared about that kind of thing. I just—"

"There's plenty you don't know about me," Cricket cries, brushing away a tear. "And you're never going to know. Because you've screwed up my life for the last time. I don't need your surfing advice. I don't need anything from you. I hate you!"

Dad looks so crushed, Cricket almost feels sorry for him. But she feels even sorrier for herself. Turning from her father, she jumps into the car and drives away.

13

Anyone interested in a sunset session at Sunset?" Luna's mother asks at dinner that evening.

"Yes!" Isobel cries. She's the big-wave surfer of the group and she's been waiting all week for a chance to tackle some truly epic North Shore surf.

"I'll go," Luna says, searching the take-out boxes that litter the table for a few more bites of Chinese food.

"Me, too," Rae agrees eagerly.

Cricket looks at Kanani. Her friend is fiddling with her chopsticks, a glum look on her pretty face. "I'll pass," she says.

Cricket nods. "Me, too." Normally, she'd love to try her hand at Sunset, but tonight she's just too depressed to care. Besides, she needs to talk to Kanani.

"Don't stay out too late," Deirdre clucks, sounding almost like her old self.

"Why?" Cricket asks hopefully. "Are you planning another photo shoot for tomorrow?"

"I wish," Deirdre replies. "Tomorrow my editor will decide if we can stay and reshoot the fashion spread, or if he's going to shoot something in California with professional models. If he chooses the second option, we'll be heading home on the next plane out of here."

"Maybe the police will recover the missing rolls of film," Cate suggests, "and then all this will be moot."

Deirdre sighs. "The cops didn't seem too optimistic. None of the residents are talking. They're covering for whoever did this."

Kanani scowls. "What makes you think it was the locals who did it?"

"Well, I can't imagine a tourist would rip us off," Deirdre replies. Then she gasps, apparently remembering that Kanani is half Hawaiian, and adds, "I'm sure it isn't any of *your* relatives who were involved."

Cricket is having trouble keeping her mouth shut. She wants to tell Deirdre that although the film might have been stolen by a local, the entire mess happened because of her father. But she's too embarrassed to admit that it was one of her relatives, not Kanani's, who screwed up the girls' modeling debut.

"Come on, girls," Cate pipes up, breaking the tension. "Let's get our boards and move out." She turns to Cricket and Kanani. "Are you sure you don't want to come? It's bound to be more fun than moping around here."

"No, thanks," Cricket answers. "I'm going for a walk on the beach. Will you come with me, Kanani?"

Kanani looks ready to say no. Then she sees the pleading look on Cricket's face. "Sure," she says, carrying her plate to the sink. "Let's do it."

"Do you realize we just gave up a chance to surf at Sunset Beach?" Kanani says as they walk up the beach toward Lili'u's Reef. "We must be insane."

"I'm too upset to surf," Cricket answers.

"Me, too. While you were jogging this afternoon, I went to the Internet café in Haleiwa. Francisco has only sent me one e-mail since I've been gone." She turns to Cricket. "He and his family went to Miami to spend Christmas with his aunt. Do you think he met someone there?"

Normally, Cricket would try to calm her friend's fears. But right now she's too involved in her own problems to help Kanani with hers. "I didn't go jogging this afternoon," she blurts out. "I borrowed one of the cars and went to see my dad."

"You went surfing?"

Cricket shakes her head. "When we were at Lili'u's Reef, Kainoa told me why the guys were dropping in on us. They found out that Deirdre plans to reveal the location of their surf spots in *Water Woman*."

"What?" Kanani gasps.

"Yeah. And you know who told them? My father."

While Kanani listens wide-eyed, Cricket tells her the

whole story. "Can you believe it?" she concludes. "Thanks to my stupid dad, someone—probably Kainoa or one of his friends—stole our film. And now we're out of the magazine and our entire trip is ruined!"

Kanani stares at her. "Wait a minute. Why are you blaming your father?"

"Who else should I blame? He could have gone directly to Deirdre, but no. Like some brownnosing teacher's pet, he had to blab everything to everyone who lives around here."

"But don't you get it, Cricket? Your dad is a visitor here, just like we are. It's only right to tell your host if someone is inviting strangers into their house."

Cricket frowns. "What are you talking about? No one is inviting strangers into anyone's house. Deirdre was going to do a little free advertising for the North Shore, that's all."

"But she promised not to reveal the name or location of Lili'u's Reef," Kanani points out. "Then she went back on her word. That's not right."

"Okay, sure. I mean, assuming my dad heard her correctly. Who knows? Maybe he'd had a couple of beers and just heard what he wanted to hear."

Kanani frowns. "You really believe that?"

Cricket remembers Kainoa's words. *"Everyone on the North Shore knows the Panther doesn't lie."* "I guess not. But look, what's the big deal anyway? So what if Deirdre writes about Lili'u's Reef in her article? The locals should be happy she's giving the tourists one more reason to visit their island. After all, tourism has made Hawaii rich."

"It's made the haoles who built the big hotels rich," Kanani retorts. "But the locals? I don't see too many of them living in mansions—except maybe my birthfather."

Cricket thinks it over. "Okay, so maybe they should try harder." It's what her mother always says about the local businesses in Crescent Cove. According to her, it's up to them to attract tourism by advertising, keeping their shops and restaurants looking good, and offering special sales and bargains for visitors. "They should open some locally run inns and shops, give tours of local Hawaiian places and teach people about their folklore, stuff like that. They could probably make tons of money if they spent a little less time 'hanging loose' and a little more time working."

Kanani stops walking. "Cricket, I wish you could hear yourself. You sound just like your mother."

Cricket cringes. Just yesterday, she'd told her father she was nothing at all like her mother. Now, she has to admit, she's almost parroting her words. What's up with that?

"Take a look around you," Kanani says. "What makes this island special? It's the beauty of the land and the sea—*aina* and *kai*. The people—the kamaaina—love the land and care for it. They aren't interested in making piles of money—not if it means handing over their island and their culture to a bunch of uncaring tourists."

"But not all tourists are uncaring," Cricket argues.

"Right. Like your father, for example. He respects the people here and their way of life. In return, they welcome him and treat him as their equal."

They walk on in silence. Cricket is so confused she doesn't know what to think. Then Kanani says, "If anyone is at fault in all this, it's Deirdre. She's not interested in Hawaii, or surfing, or even fashion. All she cares about is getting her name on a flashy, tell-all article— and she doesn't care who she has to step on to do it."

Lili'u's Reef is just ahead. "Who did Suzie say this reef is named for?" Cricket asks.

"Queen Lili'uokalani. She was the last reigning monarch of the Hawaiian Islands. She felt her mission was to preserve the islands for her fellow native inhabitants, but the U.S. government sent in soldiers to take over her palace and throw her out. Then in 1898, Hawaii was made part of the United States."

"That's not fair!" Cricket cries indignantly. "I mean, she wasn't doing anything wrong, was she?"

Kanani shakes her head. "The United States just wanted the land, that's all." She motions toward the waves. "The locals say she used to surf here."

"The queen? Here?"

Suddenly, three enormous sea turtles appear in the water. "Look!" Cricket cries. As she and Kanani watch, they disappear beneath the waves.

"They're beautiful," Kanani breathes.

"Kainoa told me he talks to his father even though

he's dead," Cricket says. She laughs uncomfortably. "He said his dad's spirit is alive in the turtles or something like that. I couldn't really make sense of it. It sounded a little crazy to me."

"It's not crazy," Kanani replies. "Kainoa knows his father is one of the *aumakua*."

"The what?" Cricket asks.

"The aumakua. Hawaiians believe that when people die they become aumakua—god-spirits. The aumakua appear to the living as animals—hawks, sharks, sea turtles, all sorts of creatures. Members of the aumakua's family can recognize their ancestor in any form, and can call on them for help in time of need."

"So you're saying Kainoa's father has turned into a sea turtle?" Cricket asks skeptically.

"I don't know," Kanani replies. "Maybe. Some kamaaina still believe in the aumakua. Some just think of it as a beautiful legend. Either way, it reminds people to respect the land. It's not only their home, it's their ancestors' home, too."

Cricket gazes at her friend with newfound admiration. "You really know a lot about Hawaii, Kanani."

"My roots are here. That's why this trip has been so special for me. It isn't because I thought I was getting my photo in a magazine. That's cool, for sure. But what really matters to me is walking on the land, swimming in the ocean, and surfing the waves. It's talking to the people, eating their food, and hearing them speak real Hawaiian words."

"But what about meeting your birthfather?" Cricket asks. "I thought that was the thing you wanted the most."

Kanani hangs her head. "It was. But I guess not everything turns out the way we want it." She shrugs. "I don't mind. Just being here is the main thing, right?"

Cricket wonders if Kanani really means that. Her words sound sincere, but her body language tells a different story.

The girls walk on. Up ahead, Cricket can see the red roof of Kainoa's house. Her heart throbs as she thinks of their meeting in the water this morning. She remembers the defiant look on his face as he said, "You take our aloha and spit on it, we're not going to take it lying down."

If Kanani is right—if Deirdre really did treat Kainoa and his friends unfairly—then his anger makes sense. Cricket wishes she could go to him and comfort him. *Not all haoles are like that,* she wants to say. *I'm not that way.* But after all that's happened, would he believe her?

Cricket searches her pockets for candy. She finds a couple of lint-covered M&M's and pops them in her mouth. The sweetness reminds her of the day she had lunch at Kainoa's house. She loved sitting on the lanai with him, gazing at the ocean and eating salty Spam moosabi.

And then she remembers Kainoa's grandmother

calling his little sister away from the water. "You see this beach?" Cricket tells Kanani. "According to Kainoa's grandmother, there's an underwater pipe out there that pumps treated sewage into the water. She says a new resort was built upstream, and now the output is so high it's dangerous."

Kanani looks shocked. "Cricket, why didn't you tell me about this before?"

"Sorry," she says. *Why didn't I tell her?* she wonders. For sure she would have been interested. If there's one thing Kanani cares about as much as surfing and Hawaiian culture, it's saving the planet. When she learns that someone is polluting—like that horse stable back in Crescent Cove that was dumping manure into a stream—she does everything in her power to stop it.

"Kainoa's grandmother says they've called the water department," Cricket continues, "but nobody will do anything because this isn't a popular tourist beach."

"See?" Kanani exclaims. "Just another example of how the locals don't get the respect they deserve."

Cricket thinks it over. Kanani is right, she decides. But what can they do about it? If the water department won't listen to the local adults, they certainly aren't going to listen to a couple of mainland teenagers.

Then suddenly, the most amazing idea pops into Cricket's head. If only she can get Kanani to agree!

"Kanani, we have to talk to your birthfather!"

"What?" she gasps.

"He writes editorials for the *Oahu Daily News*, right? Well, if he wrote one about the pollution at this beach, the water department would *have* to listen."

Kanani frowns, thinking it over. "I don't know anything about my birthfather, except that he has a nice house. For all I know, he might think ecology and conservation aren't important."

"He's Hawaiian, isn't he?" Cricket asks. "You told me the kamaaina care about protecting the land."

"Well, most of them do. But he's also a newspaper editor, and let's face it—this isn't exactly front-page news. What if he thinks a little pollution on the North Shore is beneath his notice?"

"We'll never know until we talk to him."

"Talk to him?" Kanani cries. "Are you serious? Maybe an anonymous phone call would be okay. Or an e-mail. Or maybe—"

Cricket grabs her friend's arm. "Face it, Kanani. He's not going to pay attention to an anonymous phone call. But if his daughter asks for his help, face to face, he's got to listen."

"You're probably right," she admits. "But Cricket, I . . . I'm scared. What if he doesn't want to see me? And even if he does, how do I know he'll like what he sees? I don't want to disappoint him."

"How could you do that?" Cricket asks. "You're smart, you're beautiful, and you longboard like a champion."

"But he looks so rich and sophisticated and important. I'm just a regular kid from Crescent Cove. I don't even know how to talk to him."

"That's easy," Cricket declares. "Just shift into Hawaiian Hurricane mode." That's what their friend Luna calls it when Kanani gets really intense and serious about fighting for one of her causes. When she's like that, she won't take no for an answer.

Kanani giggles. "I'll try. But I can't face him alone. You've got to come with me."

Cricket feels her heart skitter. Kanani's birthfather makes her nervous, too. But she can't let her friend down. She holds out her little finger and the two girls shake pinkies. "Let's do it!" Cricket exclaims.

14

"Isn't this the spot where we saw the mongoose?" Cricket says as Kanani steers around the sharp curves of Tantalus Drive.

Kanani nods. It's six-thirty in the morning and so dark she has the headlights turned on.

Cricket glances over at her friend. She can tell Kanani is nervous. She isn't talking much, and her hands are gripping the steering wheel like she's holding on for dear life.

"Relax," Cricket says gently. "It's going to be fine."

"Easy for you to say. You've already spent time with your father."

"Yeah, and it wasn't a walk in the park, either. But I hung in there and after a while we really started to connect."

Well, that's the version Cricket is selling to Kanani. The truth is Cricket doesn't know where she stands with her father right now. Last time she saw him, she told him she hated him. But that was because he'd screwed up her chance to appear in *Water Woman* magazine, and didn't even seem to care. Now she wonders if she should have listened to his side of the story. But who knows if she'll ever have a chance to ask him? After what she said, he may never talk to her again.

"Yeah, but you have surfing in common," Kanani is saying. "What do my birthfather and I have in common?"

"You won't know until you get to know him," Cricket replies. "Oh, there's the driveway!"

Kanani looks like she's considering driving on, but at the last minute she veers down the driveway. She stops in the same place as last time, but Cricket reminds her they aren't trying to hide anymore. "I sure wish I was," Kanani mutters, but she drives on and stops next to a green Range Rover that's parked beside the house.

"Go on," Cricket says. "Ring the bell."

"It's still early," Kanani answers. "What if he's sleeping?"

"Then you'll wake him up. Big deal. It's not every day his long-lost daughter shows up."

Kanani opens the car door, then hesitates. "I can't face him alone. Come with me, okay?"

"Well . . ."

"Please," Kanani pleads. "I'll do the talking. I just need you with me for moral support."

Cricket nods and together they climb out of the car. At the front door, Kanani rings the bell with shaky fingers. For a long moment, nothing happens.

"Maybe he's not home," she says hopefully.

Then a light goes on and Cricket hears footsteps. She glances at Kanani, who looks pale and frightened. Soon the door opens and Liko Kaunolu is standing there in pajama bottoms and a silk bathrobe. His thick, gray hair is mussed and his eyes are sleepy.

But even in his disheveled state, there's something commanding about him. He's tall—over six feet, Cricket guesses—and very handsome, with a straight back and muscular shoulders. *He looks like the Hawaiian version of the Marlboro man,* Cricket decides.

"Yes?" he says, frowning down at them. His voice is deep and resonant. "Can I help you?"

For a long moment, Kanani just stands there, completely dumbstruck. Then she blurts out, "I'm Kanani, your . . . your daughter."

Her birthfather's eyes widen ever so slightly. "What did you say?"

"I—I was born in Honolulu sixteen years ago," she stammers. "On August twelfth. My birthmother took me to California and put me up for adoption."

"I'm sorry. You must be mistaken," he says gruffly. "I don't have a daughter."

Kanani cringes at his rebuke. "My mother told me your name," she says in a halting voice. "My adoptive mother, I mean. You're Liko Kaunolu, aren't you?"

"There's been some sort of mistake," he says. "I don't have a daughter. I'm sorry, but I'm going to have to ask you to leave."

"Liko, who is it?" a woman's voice calls from inside the house.

"Good-bye," he says. Then stepping back, he quickly closes the door.

Kanani looks at Cricket with moist eyes. "Maybe I was wrong," she says. "Maybe he's not my father."

"Are you kidding? Did you see the look on his face when you told him your name? He's your birthdad, all right."

"Well, it's pretty obvious he doesn't want to admit it." She shrugs her shoulders helplessly. "Come on. Let's get out of here."

Kanani turns to go, but Cricket grabs her arm. "Not yet." Quickly, before Kanani can object, she rings the bell again.

Almost immediately, the door opens. "Girls," Liko Kaunolu says sternly, "please don't make me call the police."

He starts to close the door, but Cricket impulsively blocks it with her foot. "Mr. Kaunola, Kanani needs your help. We both do. Please don't turn us away."

"Liko," the woman's voice calls, "come back to bed. It's too early to go to the office."

His eyes dart back and forth like a cornered animal. "I'm awake now, dear," he calls into the house. "I think I'll make some coffee and check my e-mail." He steps outside and quietly shuts the door behind him. "What exactly do you want?" he asks.

"First, you need to tell Kanani the truth," Cricket says boldly. "You're her father, aren't you?"

He looks hard at Kanani, studying her face. "You have my eyes," he says at last. "And Carly's mouth."

"Is that my birthmother's name?" Kanani asks.

He nods. "She was very beautiful, just like you."

"Was?" Kanani asks. "Where is she?"

"I have no idea," he answers. "The last time I saw her was the night you were born."

"But what happened? Why didn't you keep me? Why did my birthmother put me up for adoption?"

Kanani's birthfather lets out a ragged sigh. "You're asking some very tough questions." He glances across the driveway to a banyan tree with an ornate concrete bench beneath it. "Come sit down. I'll try to explain."

Cricket holds back, but Kanani grabs her hand and pulls her along. "This is my friend Cricket," she tells her birthfather. "Whatever you have to say to me, you can say to her, too."

He sits on the bench and motions Kanani to sit beside him. Cricket stands nearby, feeling like a fifth wheel. Still, she's dying to hear what Kanani's birthfather has to say. And if her friend wants her there, well, how can she say no?

"My first wife died almost eighteen years ago," he says softly. "I was heartbroken, and so lonely I didn't know what to do. Then I met Carly." He smiles, remembering. "She was bodysurfing at Diamond Head and I almost hit her with my surfboard."

"You surf?" Kanani asks in a shocked voice.

"I used to. I haven't since Carly left. Anyway, we hit it off right away. She was studying at the university, getting her degree in marine biology. She told me she was leaving at the end of the year, but I couldn't help myself. I fell in love. I like to think she loved me, too."

"Then what happened?" Kanani asks in a whisper.

"She got pregnant. I was so happy. I told myself that now she'd stay and marry me." He looks wistfully at Kanani. "I remember the night you were born like it was yesterday. When I saw your face, I felt complete—like my whole life had been leading up to that moment." He smiles. "I named you Kanani—'my pretty one.'"

"*You* named me? But then why did you let me be put up for adoption?" Kanani asks.

"I didn't. Carly sent me home to get some rest. I shouldn't have gone, I guess, but I was so tired. When I came back, she had checked herself out of the hospital and taken you with her. I went looking for her, but she was gone—just disappeared. I never saw either of you again—until now."

"Why didn't you keep looking?" Cricket pipes up. "You could have hired a private investigator or something."

He runs a weary hand through his hair. "And drag Carly back against her will? No, she was a brilliant student and had great dreams of traveling wherever her work would take her. She made that clear enough, though I'm not sure I was listening then. If I had gone after her, what good would it have done? You can't force someone to marry when they're not ready. You can't create a loving family when one doesn't quite exist."

"I guess you're right," Kanani says, her voice catching in her throat.

"She wrote to me a month later and told me you'd been adopted by a wonderful couple. I thought of trying to find you, of hiring a lawyer and getting you back. But then I realized that you had what you needed—two stable, married parents who loved you. You didn't need me." He sighs. "In time, the pain eased. Five years ago I married a lovely woman. I never stopped thinking about Carly and you—especially you—but I had to get on with my life."

"I understand," Kanani says. "But . . ." She hesitates. "Well, you're wrong when you say I don't need you. I've been thinking and wondering about you my entire life. It's because of you I've learned so much about Hawaiian culture. It's because of you I started surfing."

"You surf?" her father says, just as shocked as she was a minute ago.

She nods. "That's why I'm here—to be photographed for an article in a surf magazine. Cricket, too. We're staying on the North Shore."

"I have to go," her birthfather says suddenly. He

starts to stand up. "My wife will wonder where I am. She's doesn't know anything about—"

"Wait!" Cricket breaks in. "You can't leave yet. We need your help."

He falls back onto the bench and stares at Cricket. It's pretty obvious he isn't used to having anyone—especially a teenager—tell him what to do. "If it's money you want—"

"Nothing like that." Cricket looks at Kanani. "Go on. Tell him."

"There's a beach near where we're staying on the North Shore," she begins. "I don't know the name, but it's just west of Lili'u's Reef. There's an underwater pipe that pumps treated sewage into the ocean. But since they've built a new resort upstream—" She glances at Cricket. "Do you know the name of it?"

Cricket could kick herself. Why didn't she ask Kainoa? "Um, uh . . ."

"I know it," Kanani's birthfather says. "It's the Opaeula Lodge."

"Since the resort opened," Kanani continues, revving into Hawaiian Hurricane mode, "the sewage output has increased so much it's polluting the beach. The locals have complained, but no one in authority is responding because it's not a popular tourist beach. That's just not right. Everybody should be able to use the ocean without worrying that the water is contaminated."

"Why are you telling me this?" he asks.

Cricket can't keep still. "You write editorials for the

paper," she says, bouncing from foot to foot. "If you wrote something about the problem, the water department would *have* to deal with it."

Kanani's birthfather narrows his eyes. "Is that why you came here?"

"That's not the only reason," Cricket explains. "Kanani wanted to meet you, but she was scared. Then we learned about the beach and I told her—"

"This is important!" Kanani cries. "More important than my little problems. If the kamaaina don't protect the land, who will?"

Her birthfather looks startled and a little impressed—like he's never seen a teenager get so worked up about the environment. Or maybe he's surprised to hear her using a Hawaiian word. "All right," he says at last. "I'll look into it."

"And write an editorial?" Kanani asks.

He stands up again. "I said I'll look into it. That's all I can promise."

He strides toward the house, but Cricket follows and catches up to him at the door. "That's your daughter back there," she says indignantly. "Aren't you even going to invite her in?"

"Look, young lady, I appreciate your concern for your friend. But you have to think about how I feel, too. I've spent the last sixteen years trying to forget I have a daughter. I haven't told anyone—not even my wife. And now suddenly, she appears on my doorstep." He shakes his head. "I'm sorry, but I'm just not ready for a full-blown father-daughter reunion. Maybe I will be someday. I don't know. But right now . . ."

He reaches for the door. "I've got to go," he says gruffly. He pauses and looks back over his shoulder at Kanani. For a brief moment, his face softens. Then he purses his lips and walks inside, closing the door firmly behind him.

15

Cricket and Kanani talk the whole way back. Did they do the right thing? Was Kanani's birthfather angry because Kanani showed up, or secretly happy? Will he ever contact her again?

"I think he just has to get used to the idea that you want to be in his life," Cricket says. "He'll come around. Wait and see."

"But he doesn't know where I live, or even where I'm staying on Oahu," Kanani replies. "Even if he wants to contact me, he can't."

"Then you'll just have to get in touch with him again. Write him a letter when you get home. Or send an e-mail. He must have an address at the newspaper."

"I can't deal with that now," Kanani says as they drive down Kam Highway. "All that matters is cleaning up the pollution at the beach. If he writes an editorial, great. If not, we've got to find some other way to make the government listen."

"But how?" Cricket asks as they rumble down the driveway to the house. "We're going home the day after tomor—"

Cricket's voice dies in her throat when she sees Cate standing in the driveway, her arms crossed over her chest. She glares at the girls. "Get out," she orders as Kanani parks the Xterra.

"We can explain," Cricket says, trying to ignore the knot in her stomach.

"I don't want to hear it," Cate snaps. "This is the second time you've taken one of the cars without permission."

Actually, Cricket realizes, it's the third, since she also borrowed one of the Xterras when she confronted her father about the lost film. But no need to tell Cate about that now.

"I'm going to leave your punishment up to your parents," Cate says. "I'm sure they'll be interested to know what their daughters have been up to."

"You're going to tell our parents?" Kanani gulps.

Poor Kanani, Cricket thinks. She got in trouble during her trip to Florida, and now she's in trouble again. Her parents are going to totally freak. But Cricket's mom? She's too busy with her job to pay much attention to Cricket. She'll probably threaten all sorts of punishments and then get busy at work and forget to follow through.

"Get inside," Cate orders. "Deirdre has something to say to you."

The girls hurry inside, expecting a second lecture.

Deirdre is sitting on the couch with Josh, her back ramrod straight and her lips pursed. Luna, Rae, and Isobel are there, too, sitting on the floor with their arms wrapped around their knees.

"Oh, there you are," Deirdre says impatiently as Cricket and Kanani join their friends on the floor. "Okay, listen up. The police don't have any leads and it looks like our film is gone forever. I called my editor this morning and he's decided to reshoot the swimwear preview in California with professional models."

Cricket and her friends let out a groan of disappointment.

"No fair!" Rae cries.

Luna nods. "This sucks."

Deirdre claps her hands like a teacher trying to quiet a class of unruly kindergartners. "We were scheduled to fly home the day after tomorrow," she continues, "but I've managed to get our tickets changed. We leave tomorrow at five o'clock."

The girls groan even louder, but Deirdre just gets up, walks into her bedroom, and closes the door.

Everyone looks at Josh, who nervously cleans his glasses. "This isn't about you, girls," he says. "You did a terrific job. It's a business decision, that's all." As if trying desperately not to roll his eyes, he adds, "If I were you, I'd use my remaining time on the island to go surfing."

"I agree," Cate says, walking in the front door. "I'm

driving to Gas Chambers. Does anyone want to come along?"

Everyone says yes, including Cricket, but the girls' usual enthusiasm is missing.

"Why do I feel like this is my fault?" Isobel says as they walk to their rooms to get changed.

"It's Deirdre's attitude," Rae replies. "She acts like she's all put out because she has to deal with us."

"Yeah," Luna says, "it's almost as if she thinks we did something wrong."

"As if!" Isobel cries. "What? Like we stole the film or something?"

Everyone laughs and rolls their eyes. Cricket laughs, too, but inside she wonders if she should tell the girls what she knows. She wants to, but she's not sure how they'll respond. Besides, she's still not completely sure how she feels herself. Did her father do the right thing by telling his Hawaiian friend what he overheard? Were the locals right to steal the film?

Well, no, she decides, stealing is never right. But did they have any justification at all? Yesterday morning she would have said no. But after her talk with Kanani, her attitude is changing. Now she realizes that the locals don't scare tourists away from their secret spots just to be nasty. They're trying to save a little bit of Oahu for themselves—a small corner that they can keep free of tourism, development, and pollution.

Still, when Cricket tries to imagine putting it all into words, her brain goes blank. Okay, she decides, she'll talk to her friends later. Maybe on the plane home. But for now, she'll just work on making sense of it herself.

In their bedroom, Cricket and Kanani change into their bathing suits in silence. There's nothing left to say, really. Tomorrow they'll be leaving Oahu. Then it's back to real life—and all the friends and relatives who'll want to know why the girls won't be appearing in the spring issue of *Water Woman*. But for now, the waves await, offering some tiny degree of consolation. For now, there's surfing.

Three hours later, Cricket drags herself out of the Xterra. She's too tired to take her board off the car, too tired to do anything except stumble into the house. She surfed full-out today, throwing herself into each Gas Chambers breaker like a starving woman attacking a Big Mac.

In fact, she totally forgot everything her father taught her. Go slow? Listen to the wave? No way. Today's session wasn't about listening and responding. It was about shaking her fist at the universe and screaming, "I don't want to go home!"

Cricket walks into her bedroom and flops down on her bed. Soon, she's drifting off. She hears the phone ring in the distance. Then she disappears into blissful sleep.

"Cricket! Wake up!"

Someone is shaking her, pulling her back from her dream. "Go away," she mumbles. She's kissing Kainoa, and she doesn't want to stop.

"Cricket! My birthfather just called!"

Cricket's eyes pop open. "What?"

"My birthfather," Kanani repeats. "He called and told me—"

"How did he know where you were?" Cricket interrupts.

"He made a few phone calls and asked around. As he put it, 'I'm a newspaperman. I have contacts.'"

"So what did he say?"

A smile is creeping up Kanani's cheeks. "He did some investigating and he's writing an editorial about the pollution at Opaeula Creek Beach. That's the name of the place. Anyway, he said it's going to be in tomorrow's paper!"

Cricket lets out a whoop of joy. "That's awesome! See, I told you he'd help us. He really cares about you, Kanani. I know he does."

Kanani shrugs. "Maybe. He did say he's going to mention our names in the editorial and explain how we brought the problem to his attention."

"That is so cool! Now everyone will know we care about protecting the land and the ocean just as much as the locals do. And Kainoa will stop being mad at me. Maybe my dad will, too."

But can her father ever forgive her for what she said? The words still haunt her. *"I don't need anything from you. I hate you."* It wasn't true then and it isn't true now. They were just words spoken in anger, intended to punish him for his years of neglect. Unfortunately, they may have worked too well. She may have driven him out of her life forever.

"What's going on in here?" Luna asks, popping her head in the room. Rae and Isobel are with her. "You two sound way too happy."

"We are happy!" Kanani crows. "Come in. We've got incredible news."

"Mind if I listen in, too?" Luna's mom asks, walking in behind the girls. "After all, you woke me out of a sound sleep. I think I deserve some explanation."

"You do deserve an explanation," Cricket says seriously. "There's a good reason why we borrowed the Xterra, and now we can tell you what it is. Right, Kanani?"

"Right," she says, suddenly shy. "I . . . well, I found my birthfather."

Suddenly, the girls are all talking at once. "What? Why didn't you tell us?" Luna cries.

"He lives here on Oahu?" Isobel asks.

"He's a famous surfer, right?" Rae says confidently.

"No," Kanani admits. "He's a newspaper editor."

Everyone looks shocked. "Maybe you'd better start from the beginning," Cate suggests.

Breathlessly, constantly talking over each other's words, Cricket and Kanani tell the story of finding Kanani's birthfather, learning about the pollution at

Opaeula Creek Beach, and convincing him to write an editorial about it.

"That is too cool!" Luna exclaims, and everyone else agrees.

"I'm still not happy you took the car without asking," Cate says, "but I understand your motivation. I'll bet this trip has been a real emotional roller coaster for you, Kanani. I'm impressed you've been able to keep it together."

"It has been kind of nuts," Kanani agrees shyly. "But I'm not the only one who's been through the wringer. Cricket found her father, too."

"*What?*" the girls gasp, turning to stare at Cricket.

It's confession time, she realizes. But will the girls greet her story with the same enthusiasm and support they offered Kanani? Will they understand why her father told the locals about Deirdre's plan? Or will they blame him for screwing up their chance at surf-magazine stardom?

There's only one way to find out. Cricket takes a deep breath and tells all.

When she finishes, the girls stare at her in stunned silence. It's Cate who speaks up first. "I'm going to call the *Water Woman* editor and tell him what's been going on," she says. "I think he's going to be very interested to hear what Deirdre's been up to."

Why didn't I think of that? Cricket wonders. But who knows if the editor would have believed her anyway? Cate Martin, however, is a different story. She's got clout.

Cate leaves to make the phone call, and the girls turn to Cricket. "Why didn't you tell us you'd found your dad?" Luna asks.

Cricket shrugs. "It seemed like my father wasn't ready to open up completely, and I guess I was just following his lead. And then, when he overheard Deirdre at the club and told his friend about it, I was mad. I thought it was his fault the film was stolen, and I blamed him for ruining our chance to be in the magazine. But Kanani set me straight about that. My dad was just trying to do right by the local surfers. He really cares about this island, just like they do."

Just then, Cate walks back in, smiling like the cat who ate the canary. "Great news! I talked to Bob Pomerantz, the editor. He's taking Deirdre off the story. Instead, he wants Cricket and Kanani to write an article in journal format, giving their personal impressions of the trip. Not only that, but he said we can reshoot the entire fashion spread here on the island. The only catch is we have to get it done before our plane leaves tomorrow evening."

"But how can we do that?" Cricket cries. "The locals won't let us surf at Lili'u's Reef anymore."

"That might change once they find out you girls convinced the *Oahu Daily News* to print an editorial about the polluted beach. Then they'll know you're not like Deirdre. You're helping to protect the island, not exploit it."

"But what if they don't believe us?" Kanani asks.

"The editorial won't appear in the newspaper until to-morrow. If we're going to reshoot those photos, we have to get started right now."

Cate nods. "That's where Cricket's dad comes in. I'm going to find him and explain everything that's happened. Then I'm going to ask him to talk to his local friends and see if we can set things straight."

Cricket and Kanani exchange a worried glance. Will it work? Only time will tell.

Suddenly, a loud crash shatters the silence. Then Deirdre lets out a string of curse words that would make a sailor blush. The girls look at each other in alarm.

A second later, Deirdre stomps into the room, her eyes blazing. She walks up to Cate and shouts, "Thanks to you, my editor just fired me! But if you think I'm going to quietly roll over, you're wrong. I'm going to call my lawyer and sue the surfboard right out from under you. In fact, I'll do better than that. I'll make sure your face never appears in another surf magazine for as long as you live!"

Cate just laughs. "Go on and try it. But if you ask me, you're the one who's never going to appear in another surf magazine. Maybe you ought to find a sport where they aren't aware of how self-serving and un-scrupulous you can be."

Deirdre gasps like she's just been slapped in the face. "Let me tell you a little secret," she snarls. "I hate surf-ing. I hate salt water in my hair and sand in my bathing suit. In fact, I hate the sun. I've been sun-burned ever since we landed on this stupid island. I'm going to move to New York and write for a financial magazine—so that I never have to set foot outside my office!"

With that, she turns and strides out of the room. The girls stare after her in total shock. Then Cricket starts to giggle. Pretty soon they're all laughing so hard they can barely catch their breath. Cricket wipes a tear from the corner of her eye. Is she laughing or crying? She's not exactly sure. All she knows is that for the first time in days, there's hope in her heart.

16

Cricket stands on the shore in a body-hugging blue bikini, gazing out at Lili'u's Reef. Her heart is slamming against her ribs, and her stomach is twisted like a pretzel. She hugs her surfboard to her side and asks herself the question she knows all her friends are asking: *Will the locals welcome us back into the lineup? Or will they diss us like they did last time?*

Cricket waxes her board and thinks about everything that's happened since she told Cate and the girls about finding her father. First, Cate drove into Haleiwa to find Chet Connolly. When she returned, the girls gathered around, eager for news.

"I told him that Deirdre was off the story," she said, "and that *Water Woman*'s editor is committed to keeping Oahu's secret spots a secret. I also told him how Cricket and Kanani convinced Kanani's birthfather to write an editorial about Opaeula Creek Beach in the

Oahu Daily News. He said he'd spread the word and get back to us."

After that, there was nothing to do but wait. Kanani and Isobel wrote in their journals. Luna wrote post-cards, and Rae read a book. But Cricket couldn't sit still. She gulped down a whole package of Pepperidge Farm cookies as she paced the lanai.

Then finally, the phone rang. It was Cricket's dad and he told the girls to show up at Lili'u's Reef in fifteen minutes. That was it—no explanation, no reassuring words. Just show up.

So here they are, lined up on the shore with their boards at their sides—and Chet Connolly nowhere in sight. Out in the lineup, the local guys are ripping. Despite her nervousness, Cricket is seized with an intense desire to get out there. The surf is epic and she wants to charge it!

"I can't wait any longer," Rae says, echoing Cricket's thoughts. "Let's get this over with."

"We should wait for Cricket's dad," Isobel says. "Maybe he wants to talk to us."

"If he told us to meet here, it wasn't to talk," Luna declares.

Josh looks up from pulling on his flippers. "I say go for it. If we want to get these photos reshot by tomorrow evening, there's no time to lose."

"Let's do it," Kanani agrees.

With Cate at their side, the girls paddle into the channel. Cricket scans the lineup, searching for Kainoa. Is he out there? She can't see him.

But she does see his friend Palani. He's soaring across the face of a perfect six-foot slammer. Cricket catches his eye and tries a tentative smile. Palani smiles back, then disappears down the line.

Cricket's heart lifts with hope. Maybe, just maybe, everything is going to be okay. She paddles into the lineup and sits on her board. No one talks to her or even looks her way. But they're not giving her the stink eye, either, and that's a good sign.

"What do you think?" Kanani asks.

"I think I'm going to take the next wave," Cricket replies.

She glances toward the locals. When they notice her paddling into position, they hang back. Then she hears a voice cry, "Geevum, Cricket!"

She knows that voice. It's Kainoa!

Cricket drops into the wave and pulls into a strong bottom turn, body held low, knees bent. Then she charges into a spray-flinging backside snap. She's all set to pull off another when she remembers her father's words. *Listen to the wave.* So she straightens out and pulls back into the shack, watching to see what the ocean is about to offer her.

Up ahead, the wave is curling, offering a potential tube ride, or maybe a nice off-the-lip. Cricket decides to head for the lip. She plows down the line, aims for the sky, and catches the lip as it hurls forward. Suddenly, she's airborne, flying higher than she ever has in her life. In a heartbeat, she knows what the wave is telling her to do. She kicks into a 180—and lands it!

Finally, resisting the temptation to squeeze a couple more snaps out of the mush, she floats over the white-water and rides a little inside section into the shore. That's when she notices that Josh has been snapping photos of her throughout her ride. He gives her a thumbs-up sign and paddles out to shoot Luna sailing into a beautiful barrel.

When at last Cricket kicks out, she sees her father standing on the shore watching her. Instantly, she feels shaky all over. It's the first time she's seen him since she told him she hated him. How is he going to react?

To her amazement, he smiles and shoots her the hang-loose sign. Laughing with relief, Cricket responds in kind. Then Dad throws his board in the water and paddles into the channel. Cricket joins him there. Her first impulse is to talk, talk, talk—to tell him what's been happening, describe her feelings, explain why she said those rotten things to him, and reassure him she didn't really mean it.

But then she realizes that too much talk will make her father shut down. Better to just follow his advice. *"Surf first, talk later."*

So that's what she decides to do. Paddling out, she sees Kainoa take off on a wave. He grins as he cuts back, sending up a rooster tail of spray.

"Shaka!" Cricket shouts. "Geevum!"

"Where'd you learn to speak pidgin?" her father asks.

"From Kainoa."

"Oh, so that's Kainoa. I've been asking around about him. I figure if my daughter is hanging out with him, I'd better check him out."

Cricket laughs. "You sound just like someone's father!"

"I *am* someone's father. I know I haven't acted much like one, but I'm yours."

"Oh." Cricket never thought of him as *that* kind of father—the kind who worries about you, and sets curfews, and checks out your boyfriends. She's not sure if she likes it. And yet, on some level it feels good to know that he cares about her.

"What did you find out about Kainoa?" she asks.

"He's a good *kane*—a good boy. Since his father died, he works hard to help his family. He's not a bad surfer, either."

They paddle into the lineup. All the locals call out to her father.

"Panther, howzit?"

"Nice day, brah, yeah?"

"Waimea's coming up. You want we go check it out later?"

Cricket's dad has a friendly word for everyone. Then, as the next set comes in, he turns his attention to the surf. Cricket notices that the younger locals back off when the Panther paddles into position.

Dad drops in and soars gracefully across the face of the wave. Cricket's heart swells with pride as she watches. Back in California, she's heard people describe her father as difficult, eccentric, reclusive. Her mother has called him much worse. But here, in the powerful surf of the North Shore, surrounded by his friends, he seems completely at home, completely at ease. He's not an eccentric now. He's a *kahuna*—a master.

Cricket looks around and smiles. Everywhere she looks she sees her girlfriends ripping side by side with the locals. Her heart soars when she realizes she had something to do with making it happen.

Then Dad paddles back out. "You ready to take one together?" he asks.

"You and me?" Cricket asks, suddenly a jangle of nervous energy.

"Tandem. Like we old guys used to do with the girls at Malibu."

Cricket stares in disbelief. "Are you kidding?"

Dad just smiles. "Get on my board."

Cricket rips off her leash and pushes her board to Cate for safekeeping. Then she climbs on the front of her father's longboard. They both get on their knees and he paddles into a wave.

"Stand up!" he shouts as they sail down the face.

Then suddenly she feels his powerful hands grab her around the waist and lift her into the air. He holds her horizontally over his head and shouts, "Pretend you're doing a swan dive."

Cricket arches her back and spreads her arms. She's never thought of herself as graceful, but right now she feels like a ballerina. Or even better, a bird. She's soaring over the wave, sailing with it.

Josh is in the water, snapping photo after photo. Could a picture like this end up in *Water Woman*? Would Dad allow it? She doesn't know and she doesn't care. All that matters is the moment. *Now.* And this moment is definitely one of the best she's ever experienced.

Cricket is certain she could surf Lili'u's Reef all day, but at last Josh calls the girls in. "If we're going to make our deadline, we've got to get moving. The shave ice shack is our next stop."

Everyone groans, remembering how hot and boring it was posing with the untouchable shave ice. The girls dry off and raid the cooler. Cricket is gulping down a Red Bull and watching her father catch wave after wave, when suddenly she feels a hand slide gently around her waist.

She jumps, startled—and then giggles. It's Kainoa.

"Howzit, haole girl?"

"Hey, I thought I asked you not to call me that."

"I'm just teasing, yeah? Actually, you've been upgraded to malihini."

"What does that mean?"

"Newcomer. But you stay here and keep surfing with me, someday my bruddahs call you kamaaina."

"I'd like that," Cricket says wistfully. "But I'm going home tomorrow."

Kainoa's face falls. "When are you coming back?"

"I don't know. School starts up again next week."

"Same here," he says. He leads her toward the palm trees and sits in the sand, motioning for her to join him. "But pretty soon I'll graduate. Then you can come back and maybe we can open a surf camp together."

"I still have two more years of school," Cricket replies. "I'm only a sophomore."

Kainoa sighs deeply. "I'm worried I'm never going to see you again, Cricket."

"No, that's not true," Cricket insists. "I'll be back someday. And in the meantime, we can e-mail and call each other and—"

"I'll be honest with you, Cricket. I'm not one to write letters and stuff. But I'll be thinking about you, and hoping you return to the North Shore."

Cricket feels like crying. Is Kainoa blowing her off? Or just being honest? Either way, it hurts to leave him. But before she goes, there's something she has to say. She takes a breath and begins. "Kainoa, I want to thank you for all you've taught me about Hawaii. Now I understand why the land and sea mean so much to the kamaaina—and why you don't always welcome outsiders. The haoles have done a lot of damage to your culture. I see that now."

Kainoa smiles. "Yes, but I'm not one of those locals who thinks all outsiders are bad. And I want you to know, I didn't steal your film. I didn't even know it happened until today. Do you believe me?"

Cricket looks into his eyes and she knows he's telling the truth. "Yes."

"In that bikini you chicken skin kine nani. And you're also the smartest, most interesting, most special girl I've ever met."

Cricket's face feels hot and her heart is thumping like a boom box. Can Kainoa hear it? she wonders. But before she can decide, he pulls her close and kisses her.

Her boom-box heart turns up the bass, and her entire body feels like it's on fire. Boldly, she runs her hand through Kainoa's long, black hair. It's so soft, just like his lips. Then she puts her arms around him and feels his wiry muscles. The contrast just blows her mind. Kainoa is so hot!

"Okay, enough of that!"

For one small second, Cricket thinks it's her father, playing his new role as a middle-class, eight-rules-for-dating-my-teenage-daughter dad. But then she realizes it's Josh.

"Deirdre isn't on the story anymore, so it's up to me to crack the whip," he declares emphatically.

"Oh, come on, Josh," Cricket moans. "Just five more minutes."

"Not a chance. Up, girl! We've got two more locations to shoot this afternoon."

Reluctantly, Cricket scrambles to her feet. "Check the newspaper tomorrow," she tells Kainoa. "The editorial by Kanani's birthfather will be in there. I think you're finally going to get your beach cleaned up."

Kainoa gives her one last hug. "So long, my pretty malihini. Come back soon."

"I will," Cricket says. She doesn't know how or when,

but one way or another she's going to make it happen. In fact, she has a feeling deep in her heart that she's going to live on Oahu someday. With Kainoa, in a little house by Lili'u's Reef maybe?

Well, she decides, *I'll just have to wait and see.*

17

Cricket slumps in a plastic chair and gazes around the Honolulu airport terminal. She's so tired, she can hardly focus. Yesterday, after their photo shoot at Lili'u's Reef, the girls rushed to the shave ice shack on Kam Highway for another two hours of modeling. Then Josh marched them into Haleiwa for a quick dinner, followed by a few shots of the girls strolling down Main Street.

Today was more of the same—a long photo session at Kapena Falls and a second session at the botanical garden. Then they hurried back to the house, packed their stuff, and loaded up the Xterras.

Kanani plops down beside Cricket. "Thank God for Cate," she says.

Josh's plan had been to drive immediately to the airport, but Cate had insisted on one last surf session at Velzyland. With all the girls screaming enthusiastically in his ear, Josh had to give in.

"Those waves were pumping," Kanani exclaims. "And the water over the reef was like six inches deep. It was scary!"

"I know. But I figured this was my last day on the North Shore. I had to go for it."

Kanani lets out a sigh. "Our last day. I can't believe it."

Cricket sits up with a start. "Did you get a copy of the newspaper?"

Kanani gasps. "We've been so crazed, I totally forgot!"

The girls leap up and rush toward the nearest newsstand. "Where are you going?" Josh cries. "We're going to be boarding any minute!"

Cricket blows him off with a wave of her hand. She and Kanani dash into the newsstand and search for copies of the *Oahu Daily News*. At the bottom of a bin, they find two dog-eared, end-of-the-day copies. They snatch them up and each girl opens to the editorial page.

"Here it is!" Kanani cries.

"Are you girls planning on buying those papers?" the salesclerk asks, brushing crumbs from the front of her floral-print muumuu.

"Sure, sure," Cricket mutters, tossing some money on the counter. But her mind is on the editorial, which eloquently explains the problem at the beach and demands that the water department add another pipe to handle the extra sewage from the Opaeula Lodge. It also demands that both pipes be placed farther out at sea "so the treated sewage won't endanger the swimmers and surfers who enjoy the beach."

Finally, the editorial mentions that complaints from local residents have been ignored because the beach isn't a popular tourist destination. "Don't our local citizens deserve clean water, too?" Kanani's birthfather writes. "It took two young visitors to the island, Kanani Morehouse and Cricket Kavanaugh, to bring this problem to my attention. *Mahalo*, girls."

"I'm so stoked!" Kanani exclaims. "Now that this editorial is out, I bet that beach will be cleaned up in a heartbeat."

"He didn't mention that you're his daughter," Cricket says sadly. "I guess I was hoping . . ."

Kanani shrugs. "It's like he said to you—he's not ready for a full-blown father-daughter reunion. And to tell you the truth, I'm not so sure I am, either. I mean, I have two parents back in California, and I love them a lot. I don't know if I'm ready to add my birth-father to the mix." She pauses. "But you know what? This morning before we left the house, I called the newspaper and left my e-mail address on his voice mail. When he's ready to get in touch—I mean, if he ever is—at least he'll know where to find me."

Cricket gives her friend a hug. "When the time is right, I know he will."

The girls return to the gate and join their friends. "Look who's here," Rae whispers, motioning to a seat in the corner. Cricket glances over. It's Deirdre, and she's got her head buried in a financial magazine.

"She showed up right after you left," Isobel says. "I guess she couldn't get an earlier flight."

"I see she's already planning her future," Luna snickers. "*Business Today*. I don't suppose they run a spring swimwear preview in that magazine!"

"Oh, you never know," Rae quips. "Can't you just picture it—Wall Street investors in bikinis, posing on the Staten Island Ferry? Now that's what I call hot!"

The girls crack up. But soon Deirdre is forgotten and the girls begin reminiscing about their best North Shore surf moments. Kanani quickly joins in, but after a moment, Cricket wanders off. She's still thinking about Kanani's birthfather, and the fact that he didn't mention that Kanani is his daughter. He didn't invite her into his house, or introduce her to his wife, either. Still, Kanani seems to be handling it. She's got the right attitude, Cricket decides—just taking things one day at a time and not expecting too much.

Why can't I feel that way about my dad? Cricket wonders.

Their last surf session at Lili'u's Reef was awesome—especially that last tandem ride—but it wasn't enough. She wants to get to know her dad, to learn more about his past, to better understand why he's such a loner. She wants to convince him that she needs him in her life. Most of all, she wants to surf with him again.

But like Kanani, she knows she has to take it one day at a time and be grateful for what her dad has already given her. And she has to admit, it's a lot. Thanks to him, her surfing has improved outrageously. She no longer measures her rides by how much spray she throws. Instead, she's learned to slow down, read the wave, and respond.

He's also taught her not to get too carried away by the promise of surf stardom. *Sure,* she tells herself, *it's cool to get your photo in a magazine. But if you have to step on someone else to do it, it's not worth it.*

A voice over the intercom ends Cricket's musing. "Attention, please. Aloha Airlines Flight 4382 to Los Angeles is now boarding."

Cricket picks up her backpack and hurries to join her friends in line. She's fumbling with her ticket when she hears someone call her name. She looks up—and there's her father, hands stuffed in his pockets and a self-conscious grin on his face!

"Dad! What are you doing here?"

"I couldn't let you leave without saying good-bye, could I?"

Is this Chet Connolly talking? Cricket wonders. The guy who can barely get it together to send a birthday present? And now he's made it to the Honolulu airport to see his daughter off. Unreal!

Cricket steps out of line and joins her father. "It's been really cool hanging out with you, Dad," she says.

"Likewise. You're turning into a pretty decent surfer."

Not exactly the glowing praise she was hoping for,

but she'll take it. "You're not too bad yourself," she retorts.

Her father chuckles. "Listen, I'll be back on the mainland in a couple of months. I'll look you up and maybe we can go surfing." He reaches into his pocket and pulls out a bar of wax. "I brought you some more of my homemade surf wax. Don't use that store-bought junk. This is the real thing."

Cricket has a sudden inspiration. "Have you ever thought of selling your wax, Dad?"

He shrugs. "What do I know about selling stuff? I already told you, I can't get into that corporate mind-set."

"But you could just keep it small, maybe sell to a few select surf shops. Or start your own Web site. With your reputation, I bet you could attract lots of customers."

Dad laughs. "You sound like your mom." Cricket scowls, but Dad quickly adds, "I don't mean that in a bad way. The truth is, you're a little like both of us— and still totally yourself."

Cricket's heart swells with love. On impulse, she throws her arms around her father and leans her head against his chest. He hesitates a moment, and then hugs back.

"Attention, please," the voice on the intercom says. "This is the final boarding call for Aloha Airlines Flight 4832."

"Cricket, hurry up!" Kanani calls.

Cricket gives her father one last squeeze. Then she

hands her ticket to the flight attendant and follows her friends down the jetway. As she steps onto the airplane, she looks out the window. In the distance, palm trees and flowering bushes flutter in the tropical breeze. She remembers the night of the luau, when Kainoa picked a red hibiscus flower and placed it gently behind her ear.

"I'll be back, Kainoa," she whispers. "I promise."

But in the meantime, there's plenty to look forward to—her photo in the spring edition of *Water Woman* magazine, the rest of the school year, and maybe even a few California surf sessions with her weird and wonderful dad.